In the Beginning

In the Beginning

Previously titled *Dom and Va*

JOHN CHRISTOPHER

Aladdin

New York London Toronto Sydney New Delhi

ALADDIN

An imprint of Simon & Schuster Children's Publishing Division
1230 Avenue of the Americas, New York, NY 10020
This Aladdin hardcover edition May 2015
In the Beginning text copyright © 1973 by John Christopher
Previously titled *Dom and Va*
"In the Beginning" short story text copyright © 1982 by Longman Inc.
Jacket illustration copyright © 2015 by Anton Petrov
Also available in an Aladdin paperback edition.
All rights reserved, including the right of reproduction in whole or in part in any form.
ALADDIN is a trademark of Simon & Schuster, Inc., and related logo is a registered trademark of Simon & Schuster, Inc.
For information about special discounts for bulk purchases, please contact
Simon & Schuster Special Sales at 1-866-506-1949 or business@simonandschuster.com.
The Simon & Schuster Speakers Bureau can bring authors to your live event. For more information or to book an event contact the Simon & Schuster Speakers Bureau at 1-866-248-3049 or visit our website at www.simonspeakers.com.
Jacket designed by Karin Paprocki
Interior designed by Hilary Zarycky
The text of this book was set in Venetian 301.
Manufactured in the United States of America 0415 FFG
2 4 6 8 10 9 7 5 3 1
Library of Congress Control Number 2015932392
ISBN 978-1-4814-2004-4 (hc)
ISBN 978-1-4814-2003-7 (pbk)
ISBN 978-1-4814-2005-1 (eBook)

To Margaret with love

Contents

In the Beginning

Five hundred thousand years ago or thereabouts, in Africa, two different kinds of early man lived and died and left their bones, which scientists find today in the Olduvai Gorge. One race had no tools but had weapons—weapons made from the bones of the antelope, whose flesh they ate. They were hunters and fighters: killers by nature. The other race learned how to make tools out of stones. They were gentler and weaker than the hunters.

When the climate changed and the two races met at last, and fought for existence, there could be no doubt which must win.

I

FOR MANY DAYS AFTER THEY STARTED THEIR trek southward, the tribe were in familiar territory with recognizable landmarks and known water holes; but at last they came to the point, ten days' march from the Cave, beyond which they had never previously ventured. It was a small outcropping of rock, nothing to note in the vast emptiness of the grasslands and invisible fifty yards away.

There they halted, and Dom's father turned to the north, to where the Cave lay far beyond the horizon. He spoke to the spirits of their ancestors who dwelt there, telling them of his sadness at taking the tribe into the unknown lands of the south. It was a hateful thing but necessary; because year after year there had been less game, and without game the tribe could not live.

He did not ask the spirits for their protection in the future. They all knew it would have served little purpose. The protection of the spirits had power only in lands where they themselves had roamed in the flesh. Uncharted strangeness lay ahead.

Then Dom's father turned his back on the Cave, and raised his hand in signal to the tribe.

"Now we go."

Day after day they traveled south. At first the country was no different from that to which they were accustomed: rolling grassland with occasional rocks and small bushes, a few rounded hills. All that had changed was their awareness of it, the sense of familiarity. But that counted for much. A feeling of unease clung to them, bowing their shoulders and chilling their hearts despite the sun that burned from dawn to rapid dusk out of the blue arch of the sky. Children whimpered unaccountably. Hunters quarreled with one another and sometimes fought savagely.

And water holes had to be found. In the land they had known, all but the youngest children could have made their way unhesitatingly to those oases on which, even more urgently than on meat, their lives depended. The tribe could live at a pinch on roots, if need be go for days with empty bellies, but without water they must die.

They searched and found them, following signs—tracks of animals, a bird distantly hovering, small changes in the pattern of vegetation—but it was not easy, and they learned to live with thirst. In addition the searching took up time which otherwise could have been devoted to the hunt.

Game remained scarce. The herds of antelope they discovered were few and small. They hunted them and occasionally made a kill and filled their bellies, but more often than not they went hungry; and hunger increased the unease which racked them. They feared this alien land.

Then one day they met strangers.

The first encounter was at a water hole. They had gone there following a kill and the hunters were resting beside the pool. There were hills nearby, peaked with jagged rock. One of the women called out, pointing to the figure that stood on the ridge above them.

It was a man who wore skins as they did and carried a club. From this distance his features were indistinguishable: he might have been one of themselves. But Dom, hearing the low growl of anger that swelled from the throats of the other hunters, felt the hair prickling on his head. He growled himself with the beginning of rage, and his heart beat faster.

Dom's father gave a command and the hunters moved, but they needed no urging. They raced up the ridge toward the stranger, yelling their hatred, and the old ones and the boys followed after them, shouting more shrilly. When the stranger fled their shouts grew louder and more savage.

The chase led them in the direction of the hills. The fleeter-footed of the hunters were gaining on the man as he reached the first rocky slope and scrambled up it, scattering small stones. The slope leveled to a rugged plateau, about a hundred yards wide, then rose more steeply. They saw him run across it and shouted in anticipation of triumph. On the second steeper slope the rock was bare of grass or plants, and higher up Dom saw the openings of caves. It was toward them that the stranger was climbing.

Figures emerged from the openings and the hunters yelled with sharpened anger. They flung themselves at the second slope, using their clubs to get purchases in clefts of rock, pulling themselves up with their free hands. The men of the other tribe, standing above them, shouted in reply. The words in themselves meant nothing but what they conveyed—rage and defiance—was plain enough.

Dom's father was in the lead, Dom behind him to his right. He had no thought of what might happen when they came to grips with these others, beyond the awareness that they were enemies and so must be killed.

Then the rocks began to hurtle down. He thought the first one had been dislodged by accident but it was followed by a second, by a shower of rocks. Near him a hunter cried out and fell backward. Dom looked up and saw one of the enemy, standing on a ledge, hurl down a boulder as big as an antelope's skull. It would have hit him if he had not flattened himself against the rock face in time and seen it go bouncing and crashing down the slope.

A second hunter fell, and a third. The enemy shouted more loudly, and there was something in their cries which began to chill his blood. He saw his father get as far as the first ledge, on which the man who had thrown the boulder stood; now he swung furiously with a club. He stood half a man's height above Dom's father and the blow landed: not cleanly but with power enough to send him tumbling backward. When the other hunters saw that, they retreated and Dom went with them.

They collected together at the foot of the slope. One of those who had fallen had an arm that hung loose and his face was twisted with pain, but the rest were not badly injured. Dom's father, though he had taken the blow on his shoulder, showed only the small cuts and abrasions of his fall.

High above, the enemy chanted in triumph. They stood outlined on the ledges below the caves, and Dom could see that there were fewer of them than the hunters of the tribe—scarcely half as many. His father looked up, too, silently for a moment while the hunters watched him. Then with a frightening yell that echoed among the rocks he started to climb again.

Stones and boulders crashed down as Dom and the hunters followed him. One caught Dom on his right arm and the club almost fell from his suddenly nerveless hand. This time fear was already in his mind, not far beneath the anger. He clung to the rock face, irresolute. As he prepared to climb again he saw the hunter above him struck by a stone just above the eyes. He fell with a screech of agony, his body dropping through the air only a foot or two from Dom, hit a needle of rock and fell once more, silent now, to lie unmoving on the ground below.

That was when fear overcame anger. Dom scrambled down, concerned only to get away from the hail of stones. He had reached the foot of the slope before he realized he was not alone. Others of the hunters had fled with him and more were follow-ing suit; last of all his father.

The enemy yelled but the hunters were silent. They picked up the one who had fallen, though he was plainly dead, and went away. As they descended the second slope toward level ground, the enemy came pouring down and across the plateau to jeer at them. The hunters slouched back in the direction of the water hole. One or two moaned from their wounds; otherwise they walked in silence. The old ones and the boys, who had waited at the foot of the hill, followed dejectedly.

Dom slept badly and from the sounds about him knew that the others were as restless. In the morning they fed on what was left of the previous day's kill. Normally this would have cheered them up but it was not like that today. The hunters grumbled sullenly among themselves. At last one spoke out:

"We must go back. These are bad lands. We must go back to the Cave, to the place where the spirits of our forefathers will protect us."

He was a big man, almost as big as Dom's father. He had grumbled before but not in the presence of the chief. Dom's father said:

"That would do no good. In the old lands there is little game and the water holes are drying up. We must go on."

"But this land takes our courage from us," the hunter said, "and the strength from our arms. You go on. We will go back."

Dom's father walked stiff-legged toward the hunter and, standing in front of him, roared out his anger. It was a fearful sound and Dom shivered to hear it; but the hunter shouted back defiance. Then each took an antelope-horn dagger from his belt.

The hunter moved, making a circle about Dom's father, his heels raised clear of the ground as he walked. Dom's father turned with him, not moving from the spot on which he stood. The roaring and shouting were finished—they stared at each other in silence, lips drawn back in snarls of hatred.

After the first circle the hunter made a second, and a third. Still Dom's father turned and kept his ground. All the tribe watched, the hunters quiet, the women and boys making low hissing noises between their teeth. Dom watched too, in excitement and anger and fear.

The hunter attacked. He threw himself forward with a shriek that split the air, his right hand raised to plunge the dagger into Dom's father's neck. But Dom's father's own right arm went up, inside the descending one. The two figures met in shock. For a moment or two they swayed together, their strengths opposing and balancing; until with a cry of triumph Dom's father thrust forward and the hunter staggered and fell to the ground.

He was not hurt, although his dagger had dropped from his hand. Yet he made no attempt to rise or defend himself, not even when the weapon hand of his adversary plunged down toward him. He only groaned as the dagger stabbed through his flesh and found his heart.

Dom's father put his foot on the body, and looked at the tribe.

"We go on," he said.

They murmured in agreement. Dom's father pointed to the body of the hunter who had been killed in the attack on the hill tribe. It had been kept within the circle of sleepers all night, to protect it from scavenging beasts.

"He will stay here," Dom's father said. He rolled the other one under his foot. "As this will. Their spirits will attack our enemies after we have gone."

So the old ones took the corpses and threw them in the water hole. Then the tribe resumed its march.

The grasslands gave way to higher ground on which there were some bushes and eventually trees. They still did not see many antelope but there were other animals. They saw a giraffe for the first time, and gazed in astonishment at this huge creature with the tiny head perched on top of the long mottled neck.

The hunters gave chase and the giraffe fled away, moving awkwardly and less fast than an antelope but easily outdistancing its pursuers. The next day, though, they sighted two, and tracked them and drove them into the reach of the waiting warriors. One of the beasts lumbered toward Dom and he swung his club at a long spindly leg. His blow glanced off but others succeeded and the giraffe, with a crack of bone, crashed to the ground. The hunters threw themselves on it, driving their daggers in at a dozen different spots as the animal struggled under them. Its heart was less easily found than the heart of an antelope, and it was a long time before it lay still.

When they had feasted on the giraffe they went on. This was altogether better land; greener and with more game in it. Water holes were more frequent, too. One day they came to a small river, and stared at the broad track of water, continually running away and yet continually replenished.

One of the men said: "We could hunt on either side of this water. There is much game." He nodded to Dom's father in token of respect. "You have brought us to a good land, chief. Let us stay here and go no farther."

But Dom's father said: "In our old land we had the Cave." He pointed at the sky where, for some days past, the blue had been largely hidden by fleecy cloud. "Where will we find shelter here, in the time of rains? We must go on."

That night, as though the spirits of the sky had listened to his words, it rained: a downpour which soaked through the covering hides and drenched them all. The next morning they shivered until the sun broke through and dried them. They went on, to the south.

They came across plenty of game, of many different kinds: pigs and baboons and smaller animals like porcupine. They found zebra and hunted them, but the zebra kicked their way through the line of waiting hunters, leaving two wounded and one dead from the blows of hooves. After that they left the zebra alone and tackled easier quarry.

They did not discover a place to shelter them from the rains but the hills became steeper and rockier and Dom's father said they must find one soon.

No one disputed this. They were grateful and honored him for bringing them into a land so rich in water and game.

One night they slept near the entrance to a valley that was part grassed and part wooded. Blue-white rocks showed among the vegetation that covered its slopes. They had made a kill the previous afternoon and today, Dom's father said, they would explore the valley walls and seek a cave.

The path they took was along the western side of the valley, through scrub and treeland interspersed with clearings. Some of the boys ran ahead but Dom walked behind with the men, remembering he was a hunter and had a hunter's dignity to maintain.

Then two boys came hurrying back and went to Dom's father, nodding their heads in respect.

"We have found game!"

Dom's father said: "We do not need game. Our bellies are full, and the women carry fresh meat."

"There are strange men who are with the game."

Dom's father glared in anger.

"Hunters?"

One of the boys said: "They do not hunt. They watch."

Dom's father shook his head. Dom did not understand this, either. The watching must be part of a hunt; but the boy had said the men were *with* the game. It made no sense.

Dom's father said: "Show us this—the game, and the men who watch."

Guided by the boys the hunters went stealthily through the bushes. They came to a clearing and peered from behind a screen of leaves. They saw cattle in front of them—animals as big as the large antelope but thicker and clumsier in body. They could not run as antelope ran, Dom thought, with legs like that. When they fled, the hunters would catch them without much difficulty.

He saw the men also. There were two of them, standing near the cattle and talking together. He felt his blood stir, the hair on his neck bristling with anger.

Dom's father yelled in rage and all the hunters yelled with him. They broke shouting from the bushes and ran through the grass—the two men turned and fled but strangely the animals stayed where they were, not scattering until the hunters were among them and clubbing them down. There were more than a score and they left three dead behind; the hunters could have killed twice as many with little extra effort.

His foot on one of the beasts, Dom's father roared to the sky his triumph. All the hunters shouted, too, praising him. He had brought them through bad lands to a place where there was water everywhere, to a place where game stood unmoving while you slaughtered it. Soon he would find them a cave where they could shelter from the rains. The enemy had fled at his first cry. This was good land; and the tribe were masters of it as once they had been masters of the grasslands.

Dom shouted with the rest, proud of the tribe and of his father who had done all these things.

They feasted in the clearing which had a stream running beside it. The women cut up the dead beasts but took only the tenderest parts of their flesh: there was far more meat here than they could eat in several days. They stripped off the hides but left the bloody carcasses in the grass. Vultures circled overhead, but dared not come down while the tribe was there.

It was late afternoon and they dozed, full-bellied, in the sun. Dom had a dream of hunting, and his body twitched as in the dream he yelled at onrushing antelope. But the yell became real, echoing in his ears though not from his own throat. Bewildered he leaped to his feet and saw the enemy bursting out of the bushes on the far side of the clearing. His club of bone lay at his feet; quickly he picked it up and ran forward with the other hunters to take up the challenge.

The strangers outnumbered the hunters, though they were smaller and slimmer men. They carried pointed stones which they tried to use as daggers; but the great clubs of the hunters struck them down before they could come to grips. One of the men rushed at Dom while he was off guard from striking at another, but Dom saw him in time and fended the blow off with his arm. The man was fully grown and bigger than Dom, but he did not press the attack and fell back weakly.

The fight was quickly over, with the rest of the enemy fleeing as the first two had done. The hunters pursued them a little way into the bushes, but they ran well and the hunters were gorged with meat. They went back to the clearing where the remainder of the tribe waited.

Now their joy, and their pride in themselves and their chief, were greater than ever. By overcoming this enemy they had avenged the defeat on the rocky hillside. They had said the tribe were the masters of this good new land: their victory proved it true.

2

THAT NIGHT A LION, COUGHING IN THE distance, wakened Dom from sleep. Automatically his hand went to the club that lay beside him, to the dagger in his belt. Having checked that his weapons were within reach, he was content.

But the sound, in the stillness of the night, made him remember another such occasion. That had been in a different land, hundreds of miles to the north, and although only a few months since, in a different age. It had been the last night of his boyhood.

He remembered his fear at the lion's roar. It had

happened once that a lion had leaped the outer guarding line of hunters and snatched a child and got away with it before the hunters were properly alert. That had been an accident, all the hunters said, because in truth the lions feared the tribe. A week later the hunters killed a lion and said it was the lion which had stolen the child: the tribe, not the lions, were masters of the grassland.

But nevertheless Dom had shivered, and pulled his covering of antelope hide tighter around him. At that moment he heard his mother's voice whisper:

"Dom. . . ."

"I am cold," he whispered back.

"Come to me."

He hesitated. He was no longer a child, to be nursed. In the hunt he went out with the men, as one of the beaters who drove the antelope to where the hunters waited. In a year's time he might be a hunter himself and wield a club.

His mother said again: "Come, Dom."

Her voice was low. Dom listened and heard only the soft sounds of sleep from the others. The lion spoke again, a double cough and nearer. Slowly, cautiously, he crept toward her, and her arms found him and pulled him close. Her body was warm. Gradually his shivering ceased and he slept.

Dom remembered the following day also. In the morning the sun woke them, rising hot above the level plain. The people of the tribe got up from the nests of grass in which they had slept and moved down the slope to the water hole. They went in their customary order, with the young hunters in front and the older hunters, ranged about Dom's father, bringing up the rear: only in attack did he lead the way. In between walked the women and children and the old ones. The hunters carried only their weapons—the others carried hides and sun-dried meat. These were all the possessions the tribe had.

There was a lion at the water hole—perhaps that which Dom had heard in the night—and various small animals and birds. There were no antelope. The birds rose in the air and the animals fled as the tribe approached, the lion last of all but long before they were there.

At the water's edge the young hunters stood to either side, and the women and children and old ones made way too for the older hunters. They in turn made way for Dom's father, who strode through their ranks, biggest and strongest of all the tribe, and squatted beside the pool. He drank deeply and slowly, pausing several times before he stood up and raised his hand. Then the older hunters drank, followed by the young hunters and at last the women and children and old ones.

After drinking they ate, chewing on the dry stringy meat. Then Dom's father spoke.

"There is less water here. This pool is drying up, as others have done. The antelope know this: that is why they have gone away."

The water hole lay in a hollow, bringing the grassy horizon close on every side. He pointed to the south.

"We must follow the antelope. Wherever they go, we will go, to the earth's end if need be. But first we must go to the Cave. We will say good-by to the spirits of our ancestors, and pray to be guided to where the antelope have gone."

They listened to him, troubled but acquiescent. It was hard to imagine going into another land than this one they were used to, but they knew he spoke the truth—about the drying pools and the vanishing antelope. And they knew he was the chief.

His gaze settled on one face. He looked at Dom.

"It is time for my son to choose his weapons."

Dom's mother stood close by. She said:

"No!"

Dom's father looked at her but he did not speak. There was fear in her face. Yet she said:

"He is too young. It lacks a year before he should take weapons. He is not strong enough to be a hunter."

Dom's father took a step forward and his right hand moved. She tried to dodge the blow but his fist struck her jaw and she fell. She lay moaning at Dom's feet.

His father said to Dom: "You are my son. We must leave this land, to follow the antelope. We will go a long way from the Cave, and may not return to it in my lifetime. So you must choose your weapons, and become a hunter."

The hard eyes stared at Dom from the bearded face. There had been other sons, two of them, but they had met their deaths in the hunt. Only Dom was left.

He bowed his head in silence. His mother still

moaned as she lay on the ground, but he did not move to help her. The chief's word and wish were law to all the tribe, and especially to his son.

He remembered how after that they went to the Cave.

In the morning they could see the hills, heat-hazed above the shimmering plain, but it was late afternoon before they reached the first outcroppings of limestone, and evening by the time they came to the Cave itself. At the sight of it the tribe halted and stood silent, while Dom's father made obeisance to the holy place and to the spirits of their forefathers. Only to these would he ever bow his head.

The Cave was the one fixed place, the only thing real and distinctive among the featureless expanses of the savanna; where nests of grass were made each night and abandoned and forgotten next morning, where even the drinking holes were scarcely distinguishable one from another. In the rainy seasons the tribe moved into the Cave and lived there; if home had had any meaning for them it would have been this. Yet also it was a place of awe. Dom felt a shiver in his mind as they moved up the rocky slope that led to it.

The rock face was sheer and high, blue-white in color, pockmarked with holes. The Cave was the biggest of these. At the entrance the top of its arch was more than five times the height of a man, its width even greater. Inside, the ground was rough, littered with boulders, but the central path that ran back, sloping slightly upward, was smooth—polished by the bare feet of the tribe through many generations.

Fifty feet from the entrance was the pool. Water dripped from the wall, in a continual trickle and splash, and filled a basin several feet across. The basin was always full—even when the water holes out in the savanna dwindled, the level of the water here did not change. This wonder was caused by the spirits of their ancestors, the old ones said.

Beyond the pool the Cave forked, the smaller branch turning right and curving back on itself, its gradient still upward. This was where the tribe lived during the rainy seasons. To the left, though, the rocky slope fell away. Dark though it was, some light filtered in from outside and Dom saw the glimmer of white within. This was the Place of Bones.

• • •

He remembered also his father's words to him next morning.

"The time has come for you to be a hunter, and each hunter must find his own weapons. In the hunt his club will be a part of his arm, his dagger part of his hand as the lion's claw belongs to the lion's paw. You must choose well and no one can do the choosing for you. Only the spirits of our fathers' fathers may help you. Ask that of them, but do not disturb their rest. Go, then."

The tribe watched in silence as Dom went down the slope into the Place of Bones. He was afraid, more afraid than he had ever been in his life, but he walked steadily, knowing that fear is the first thing a hunter must learn to master.

Down the center of the cavern the heaped bones formed a ridge higher than a man and extending a long way back. For hundreds of years, thousands maybe, the tribe, when they had stripped hide and flesh from the carcasses of their kill, had brought the bones down here. Dom did as the old ones had told him and stood a long time with his eyes tight closed. When he opened them the white shapes glimmered a little more clearly. He walked beside the ridge, searching. Occasionally he pulled out a bone to examine it, and others rolled away with a dry clatter.

As a hunter he needed two weapons: a club and a dagger. Both were provided by the skeletons of the antelope. For the club he required a thighbone, and for the dagger a fragment of skull with the pointed horn. On the choice might depend not only his prowess as a hunter but his very life.

After long searching Dom found a thighbone that would do and hefted it in his hand, feeling the weight that pulled at his muscles yet added to their strength. It seemed heavy, though light compared with his father's club which he had to strain to lift. He put the bone to one side and looked for a dagger. He was pleased with what he found—a horn, easily detached from the shattered skull, whose sharpness pricked his finger. His task was completed and he could leave this place which troubled and frightened him. To go farther would mean entering the domain of the spirits, at whose threshold he now stood.

He lifted the thighbone he had found and swung it. He hesitated, then put it down and went on deeper into the cavern, searching still. At last he found what he wanted—a thighbone longer and thicker than the first. Raising it, he felt its dragging weight.

Now he was inside the domain of the spirits. Apart from the heaped mound in the center there were other bones, lying in a long line against the wall. Any of the tribe who died within a day's march of the Cave was brought to this spot to rest forever. The skeletons stretched away into distant blackness.

Dom bowed his head. He took the dagger from his belt and showed it to them, strained to lift the club high.

"Protect me," he prayed, "as I shall protect the tribe."

The skeletons stared sightlessly back at him. Thankfully Dom turned and climbed the slope, toward the light and the waiting tribe.

There was sand outside the Cave. Dom spent all day there, polishing the thighbone to brightness and honing the dagger point. As the sun was setting his father came to him.

"Are the weapons good?" he asked.

Dom stood up and silently handed him the

dagger. His father studied it carefully, trying its point against his arm, the palm of his hand.

"It is good," he said, and gave it back.

Dom gave him the club. His father lifted it and swung it. He tossed it from his right hand to his left, and back again.

"A good club also," he said, "if you have the strength to use it."

Dom did not speak. His father threw the club and he caught it, but the weight pulled down his arm.

"Mek chose a heavy club," his father said.

Mek had been his father's first son. He had been killed by the trampling hooves of a buffalo within a year of becoming a hunter.

"But you have chosen," Dom's father said, "and a choice once made cannot be altered."

Dom remembered the tribe's last hunt in the old land.

The herd of antelope was very small: consisting only of a buck and five does. The old ones and the boys set off on either side, in two separate lines, moving in the direction of the herd but fanning away at oblique angles. After fifty yards one in each line halted and the rest went on. Although the greatest risk was of being scented, they moved very stealthily, crouching low, their progress soundless except for the tiny rustle as the long grass parted for them. Two more halted, and then two more.

On previous occasions, Dom had been one of the beaters. Now he stood with the hunters at the mouth of the funnel which the old ones and the boys were forming around the grazing antelope. He touched the dagger in his belt, silently hefted his club.

Time passed slowly. As the lines moved out, dropping their sentinels every fifty yards, they must also go more cautiously. Once abreast of the prey, any slight gust of wind could carry a scent inward and alarm them. Often enough the tribe had seen their quarry take fright and flee away on springing legs into the trackless savanna.

Sweat ran down Dom's legs and his back. The muscles of his legs tightened and his fingers clenched into a fist. Behind him he could hear his father's steady breathing: he did not look round but braced his legs so that he would not tremble. Sometimes, though not often, a young hunter showed himself a coward in this test. Then the tribe cast him out, leaving him to wander alone until starvation or the lions ended his misery. Outside the tribe there was only death.

Suddenly from the distance came a shout, the wild cry of the chase, and the antelope lifted their heads and ran from it. As they ran the sentinels along either line took up the cry in turns, moving inward and driving the fleeing animals toward the hunters.

Toward Dom; for while the rest kept their places he advanced as was required of him. They were the large antelope, not the small species, and although the herd was few in number they were a fearsome sight as they raced through the grass, their hooves making the ground shake beneath his feet. He shouted, giving the hunter's cry for the first time, using his voice to force strength into his limbs, courage into his spirit. The doe . . . in the lead, a little to the right of the others . . . he chose that one. His club of bone was heavier than ever as he ran, lifting it to strike.

Then the antelope were on him. He swung the club high, aiming for the left side of the doe's skull.

But as he leaped in the air, giving himself leverage for the blow, he knew he would not strike truly. The club slid away from the animal's neck and, off balance, he fell.

Falling, he saw the buck, running in the rear of the pack. Its horns, even bigger than that one which had provided his dagger, gleamed in the sunlight. He saw the flash of hooves and knew that in a moment they would trample his helpless body; but in that moment he was overleaped. His father's voice bellowed in rage, and his father's great club smashed in an arc through the sky and crashed down behind the buck's left horn.

The buck's front legs crumpled as the hooves were almost on Dom. Its head dropped like a rock on his chest, driving breath from his body. As he struggled to free himself he saw the great brown eye of the animal close to his own, still unglazed but fixed in death.

His father pulled the antelope's head away and Dom got up, gasping and afraid. He had escaped death but he had not struck his beast truly—to that extent he had failed in the test. He stood before his father, expecting a blow.

"The club is too heavy for you," his father said. "You have not strength enough to use it."

Dom dropped his head in acceptance, but his father turned away. He placed a foot on the body of the dead animal and gave a deep roar of triumph. The tribe gazed at him in reverence.

Now the women skinned the dead buck and cut it up. They used daggers of antelope horn and knives made from the lower jaw of the small antelope, the rows of teeth honed to fine edges during the long days of the rainy season in the Cave. The implements were poor for such a task but they had learned their skills over many years: a girl of less than four worked beside her mother, using her own small knife.

A ceremony followed. Dom's mother took the liver of the antelope and offered it to his father. She cut a piece and gave it to him and he chewed it with satisfaction.

Such was the custom: the presentation of the choicest morsel from the kill to him on whose leadership and wisdom and strength the safety of the tribe depended. The second piece should go to that hunter whose club had felled the beast.

But in this kill the chief himself had struck the crucial blow—there was no one to share the glory or this succulent tidbit. The others watched as he ate, glad to see him gaining new strength from the flesh of his victim. Dom watched also, scarcely feeling hunger, though it was many hours since he had eaten and his stomach growled its need.

His father called to him, and he went forward cowering. The blow would come after all, a punishment for his failure. But his father did not strike him; instead he called to Dom's mother who held the liver in her hands.

"Give it to him also," he said. "My son is a hunter. He needs strength to swing his club, and will get it from this meat."

So his mother gave Dom a piece of the liver. The rich smell made his nostrils twitch, and saliva flowed in his mouth. Fearful that the gift might be taken back, he wasted no time but bit deeply into its softness. Blood ran down his jaws as his mother and father and all the tribe watched him eat.

All these things Dom remembered as he lay surrounded by the tribe in the valley, a quarter of a mile from the scene of their victory. The lion coughed again, farther off, and he thought of it with indifference, almost with contempt. The tribe had been masters of the grassland, and were masters here.

And he, Dom, was a hunter, with strength now to wield the club he had found in the Place of Bones. A hunter and son of the chief, and perhaps in time chief himself. Contentedly he turned over and went to sleep.

3

THE VILLAGE CONSISTED OF A DOZEN HUTS, surrounded by a substantial thorn hedge. The space which the hedge enclosed was circular and about a hundred yards across; the hedge itself was made up partly of rooted living bushes and partly of dead thorny branches which had been brought into the circle to fill the gaps. These branches had been knotted into each other, tied with ropes of dried grass and reinforced with boulders, so as to make a strong and prickly wall that was several feet thick and taller than a man.

At a point where a track led up to the hedge,

there was an opening which was sealed by thorn branches backed by a large stone. The stone could be rolled away and an entrance created, but only from the inside. When the branches and the stone were in place, the wall was as stout there as it was anywhere.

These were things which the tribe discovered bit by bit. When they stumbled on the village, an hour after they set out down the valley next morning, the hunters took it first for no more than another thicket of thorn, and would have gone on past it without looking more closely. But one of them noticed the track, the line worn bare through the grass by passing feet, and they followed it. As they got closer to the hedge they could see there was an open space within, and they could also see the tops of the huts.

These they found very strange. They were some kind of tree, Dom thought at first, but unlike any tree he had ever seen. They were impossibly thick, for one thing, although not very high, and the broad glossy leaves lay flat across their tops. When the hunters went right up to the hedge, it was possible to see through, though indistinctly. Dom saw a man, and then another, come out of one of the things he had thought were trees, through an opening in the side.

The rest of the hunters had seen them, too, and automatically growled in anger. Then they saw something else, and as involuntarily backed away: inside the hedge, between the tree-caves, a plume of smoke rose into the sky.

They knew what smoke was—the herald of fire. And fire was the destroyer that every now and then, in the dry seasons, had swept across the parched grasslands, driving animals and men in flight before it. Its flaming teeth devoured the land, leaving a blackened desolation behind. All the animals feared fire, and the tribe feared it no less.

Having retreated, the hunters came together again some twenty yards from the hedge. They were prepared to fly but needed to see which way the fire was likely to move so that they could run the other way along the valley. There was very little wind—the column of smoke stood up almost straight—so they got no help from that.

But the column of smoke did not move, and grew no bigger. At last, led by Dom's father, the hunters lost their fear also. They could see other men beyond the barrier of thorns. They were in there, along with the fire, and seemed to have no fear of it. Realizing this, the hunters' alarm disappeared.

For this clearly was the place in which the tribe who had attacked them while they were feasting lived, and they, as the event had shown, were cowards and weaklings. The hunters once more growled with anger. Dom's father stood close to the hedge and roared his defiance. He shouted at the men inside:

"This land is ours! We are the masters here as we were of the grasslands. You are nothing but women! You attacked us without warning but we drove you away with our killing clubs. Two you left dead when you ran from us. Come out of hiding if you are men, and we shall slaughter the rest of you. But you are not men! You are no better than monkeys, hiding behind thorns."

Dom could see a score or more of men now on the other side of the hedge. They shouted back at Dom's father, but their voices were not as deep or strong. They used words that could not be understood, words as meaningless as the howls of jackals.

But they stayed behind the protection of their hedge, and the hunters grew more and more angry.

Dom's father struck at the hedge with his club, trying to break it down: the branches of thorn splintered but did not give way. Other hunters did the same, with no better success. One, enraged, tried to force a way through using his arms and legs; but the thorns bit into his flesh and he fell back, discomfited.

About that time the first stones were thrown. One struck a hunter on the side of his face and he yelped with pain. They saw that some of the enemy had clambered up on top of nearby huts, and from those vantage points were hurling stones across the hedge at the hunters. The stones were quite small, of a size to fit a man's fist, but they threw them accurately. Dom's leg was cut; the wound was not deep but the blood flowed freely.

The hunters picked up some of the stones and threw them back, but the enemy, on top of the huts, had the advantage of height as those others had done on the hillside. And they were better throwers and had a better supply of missiles—others were passing stones up to them on the roofs while the hunters had to grub about in the grass, and as like as not be hit while doing so. After a time the hunters backed away, out of throwing range.

They were not downcast, as they had been following the battle on the hillside, but angry. After all they had fought these men the previous day, and easily put them to flight. If they could only get at them, if they could get across the barrier of thorns, they would destroy them. And the barrier in itself was a mark of the enemy's fear, a tribute to the might of the tribe.

But first they must find a way of getting past the thorns. Led by Dom's father the hunters circled the hedge. They learned that it went all the way round the village, without a break, and as they went round on the outside, the enemy kept abreast of them on the smaller circle within. Whenever one of the hunters ventured near, he was greeted by a volley of stones from the roof of the nearest hut.

The village had been built close to the eastern slope of the valley. On that side the ground rose away from the hedge, at first gently and then steeply. Dom's father led the hunters up the slope. Eventually they could look down over the top of the hedge and see the interior of the village.

They had a clear view of the huts, and of many other things besides. In one corner there were cattle, thirty or forty of them, penned in by a smaller fence of thorns. There were fowls scratching in the dust, and like the cattle showing no fear of the people around them. They saw women and children as well as men. And they saw the fire. The smoke rose from a pit dug in the ground, and figures stood close by it, unconcerned. Dom saw with amazement that the figures were women, and as he watched, one of them bent forward, into the very smoke, and threw in branches of wood.

Flame leaped up, tingeing the smoke with red, but although the hunters grunted with astonishment they were no longer alarmed. If such as these had no fear of fire, if their women even could stand right beside it, it would not frighten the hunters, either. What they felt was a renewal of rage at the sight of their foes walking about casually inside the defensive wall of thorns, and of the cattle which belonged to the tribe but which for the present were out of their reach.

A hunter picked up a stone and hurled it down in the direction of the village. Others did the same, yelling insults as they did so. The slope was strewn with stones and large boulders; Dom took one and cast it down with all the force he could muster. But although an occasional stone rattled into the thorn hedge, it only did so after first bouncing along the ground. The distance was too great and none went into the village.

"They are cowards," a hunter said, "but we cannot get at them. Let us go on down the valley. It does no good staying here."

"We will stay here," Dom's father said.

The hunters looked at him. His anger was very great and the one who had spoken quailed; but it was the enemy who had made him angry.

"We will stay," he said. "We will find some way of getting in there to kill them. Or if not we will wait until they come out."

So the tribe remained in the valley, not far from the village. They did not, of course, stay in one place all the time—except when they had lived in the Cave they had never slept two successive nights in the same spot. At night they made their nests of grass in one of the clearings, and in the morning moved away. During the day, when there was need of meat, they went in search of game: either up or down the valley, sometimes ranging into valleys beyond. At other times they went up to the thorn hedge, just beyond stone-throwing range, and hurled their threats at the enemy. This was the point to which they returned, however far they might have roamed during the hunt. It was a center for their wanderings, as the Cave had been.

Running with the hunters, a couple of days after they found the village, Dom felt pain in his leg. It was in the place where the stone had cut him, and when they rested after bringing the pig to bay and killing it, he examined the wound. The cut had partially healed but its edges were red, and the flesh surrounding it hot and tender.

That night he showed it to one of the old women, who was skilled in such matters. An evil spirit, she told him, had entered his body through the cut; probably one sent by the enemy, riding on the stone which they had thrown. There was nothing one could do about it except hope that the good spirits of the tribe's ancestors would come to his aid and destroy the evil one.

She shook her head doubtfully as she spoke. As they all knew, the good spirits dwelt in the Cave, and they had left the Cave far behind. Even in the old days in the grasslands, a wound poisoned by evil spirits had caused death as often as not; either by the poison spreading through the body or when the wounded one, crippled and so no longer able to keep up with the tribe, was left to starve or be eaten by lions.

Nevertheless she performed the appropriate ritual for him, making him stand facing north, in the direction where, so many long days distant, the Cave lay. Dom stood with legs and arms spread out, mouth open to its widest stretch, while she pleaded with the spirits, begging them to come flying over grassland and hills, to enter his body and destroy the evil spirit sent by the enemy. The tribe watched as this was done. Dom's father's face was heavy with fury.

"They have sent a spirit," he said, "to hurt my son. We will kill them all!"

That night Dom slept uneasily, his leg throbbing with hotness and pain. In the morning, although he could walk still, it was with a limp. His father looked at him closely, and said:

"You must stay here. You could not keep up with

the hunters; and anyway it is a bad thing to take an evil spirit with the tribe when we search for game. Stay here, and we will bring meat back to you."

Dom said to his father: "I can keep up with the women and the old ones. And the evil spirit in me will do no harm as long as I do not take part in the hunt."

His father stared at him hard.

"You will stay here."

Dom bowed his head. He watched the tribe move away along the valley, and felt lonely and frightened. No man, he knew, could live outside the tribe. His father had said they would return, and Dom believed him in this as in everything. But that did not remove the cold fear of being alone.

They had built their nests the previous night a mile down-valley from the village. After a time Dom made his way toward it. He was not sure why he did so, except that even the presence of the enemy seemed better than nothing. He threaded his way, warily limping, through the trees and bushes. He did not go out into the open grassland that surrounded the hedge, but watched the village from behind a screen of leaves.

Watching, he saw strange things. The tribe had moved off, as they always did, at the first lifting of the sun above the edge of the world, before its rays reached down into the valley itself. Now the sun stood up above the eastern slope and its light lay golden on the village. And Dom saw the hedge open as the branches of thorn were pulled away from inside. Figures came out, the figures of men driving cattle. Others also—men, women, even children.

Dom's anger rose, for a moment overcoming the pain in his poisoned leg. If the other hunters had been there he would have raced forward, swinging his club, weakness discounted by the strength of his hatred for the enemy. Automatically his grip tightened on the club's hilt. But despite his fury he had the sense to remain concealed; on his own he was helpless. There was nothing he could do but watch as the cattle were grazed, fodder brought in, and women and children picked berries from the bushes, pulled plants out of the ground and dug up roots. He went on watching as the slow day passed and the sun traveled across the sky to lose itself behind the western hills. He watched as the people of the village went back in with their cattle, and the opening in the hedge was closed.

In the evening the tribe returned and Dom ate the meat they brought him. He told his father what he had seen, and his father listened with anger even greater than his own had been.

"Tomorrow," he said, "when they come out we will be waiting for them. Tomorrow there will be a great killing."

So next morning the tribe did not go away but stayed close to the village. They watched from behind the screen of leaves, waiting for the hedge to open. Nothing happened. The hedge stayed as it was, and the enemy stayed behind it.

For more than an hour the tribe watched and waited. Then, impatient, the hunters went out into the clearing and hurled insults at the enemy. But the enemy paid no attention, except to throw stones if a hunter ventured within reach. In the end, still angry but with their throats dry from shouting, they gave up.

Dom's father said: "They are cowards. They only come out when we are away hunting."

"Perhaps they did not come out at all," said the old woman who had made the ritual of calling the good spirits to Dom's aid.

"Dom saw them."

"Evil spirits poison the mind as well as the body," the old woman said. "I have known wounded hunters who saw things that were not there. I remember one who shrieked that lions were clawing at him, though there was no lion near as all could see."

Dom's father looked at him. Dom said:

"It was not the evil spirit. I saw them come out through the hedge—many of them and their beasts also."

"They did not come out today," Dom's father said.

He looked at the old woman and then at Dom. After that he turned to the hunters.

"Tomorrow we hunt."

Dom's sleep was still more troubled. In a dream he followed an antelope which, at the moment his club was raised to strike, turned into a lion that grew bigger and bigger, towering up into the sky, and at last leaped on him. Its claws raked his leg and he awoke crying out and felt the pain still there—the pain of his poisoned wound. After that he could not sleep, but lay shivering in the chill of the night.

The tribe had made their nests in the opposite direction of the valley from the village, and perhaps twice as far away as on the previous night. Again they left Dom behind when they went off in the morning, telling him they would bring him back meat. He felt the loneliness and fear again, but in a different way; because now the poison seemed to be in his head. His brow ached and his thoughts were wild and would not fit together properly, and when he stood up there was a weakness in his legs quite apart from the throbbing pain. He lay down again in the grass and watched the tribe go away to the north. The spirits of their ancestors had not come to help him: that was clear. It had not really been a thing to hope for. The Cave was so far off that even if they had been willing to leave it, they could never find their way here.

He thought about going to watch the village again, to see if the enemy came out, but he felt too tired to move. And perhaps it was true what the old woman had suggested: that the evil spirit in him had told him lies and none of it had happened. He looked up at the sky past an arch of leaves, and saw the blue and green and the gold of the sun spin dizzily . . . or maybe it was not the sky but the earth spinning underneath him.

For a time he slept. What wakened him was not just the pain in his leg, but also thirst, tightening and searing his throat. He must have water. He rose unsteadily to his feet, almost fell again, but managed somehow to limp his way along.

He knew there was a pool in the direction which the tribe had taken, and he went that way. It seemed farther off than it ought to have been, even allowing for his slow and unsteady progress, with halts now and then to rest, clinging to a bush or the trunk of a tree. Then in his hazy vision he saw a particular oddly shaped rock and knew what had happened: the spirit had twisted his mind and led him the wrong way. He was not going in the direction of the pool, but south toward the village.

He could turn back, but the effort seemed too great. And it did not matter, anyway. This was a land of streams, not like the grasslands where water holes were as much as a day's march apart. Here in the valley one was bound to find water soon. So Dom staggered on. Once he fell, and lay there for a long time until thirst grew stronger than pain or weariness, and he rose again and stumbled forward.

The stream which he found at last was small and shallow, no more than a rivulet trickling over pebbles. Dom dropped and lay beside it, sucking water up into his mouth. It was cool on his skin and cool inside him, quenching the burning dryness. He drank until his belly was swollen with water, rested for a while, then drank again.

His head still ached and thoughts were disjointed and wild in his head, but gradually something penetrated through the dizziness into his consciousness—that he was lying out in the open, without either cover or protection. He would be easy prey to a marauding lion, or to the men from the village if they came this way. He could not be very far from the village, and he knew he was too weak to defend himself even if there were only one of them.

Yet he did not want to leave the stream—thirst grew in him again as he thought of this. He looked up and saw that it flowed downhill, out of a wood. There would be cover there, and relief from the burning sun. Awkwardly Dom got to his feet, and staggered up the slope.

Leaves first freckled and then hid the sun, and he moved into a cool darkness of green. He thought of dropping where he stood, of lying and sleeping beside the singing stream, but instinct commanded him to go farther in, for greater safety. His feet splashed through the water and small branches whipped stingingly against his face.

Gradually the going became easier. There were more trees and fewer bushes, and he could walk for the most part unimpeded. He wanted to rest again, but despite his dizziness he could hear a different sound of water somewhere ahead, and he wanted to see why. He found a bigger, deeper-channeled stream, from which the one he had been following ran away. It accounted for some of the difference in the sound, but not all. Dom walked beside the new stream, following it down, and stopped when he came through a screen of bushes hung with scarlet flowers. The mystery was solved: ahead of him the stream fell over a ledge of rock into a pool.

But there was something moving in the pool. An animal, he guessed, and his fingers tightened on the club which, despite his weakness, he had not stopped carrying: a hunter who laid down his club was dead, or soon would be. The shape moved, pale brown in the darkness of the water. It was not an animal after all, Dom saw with surprise. It was a girl.

Even though his sickness had made him come clumsily through the bushes, without a hunter's proper stealth, she had not heard him. The sound of the water must have prevented her doing so. He realized something else: that the girl in the water was making sounds herself. They were strange—not talking, nor cries of pain or fear. It was a happy noise, sweet to the ear.

He watched her use her arms and legs to move through the water, as though she were a fish or a frog, and was fascinated by it. She went to the edge of the pool and pulled herself out by grasping a jutting spur of rock. She still had not noticed him standing there and she walked over the grass to a spot where blue and white flowers grew thickly. She picked several and twisted them together into a circlet and put the circlet on her head. Then she returned to the pool and sat there, looking at the reflection of her head and shoulders in the water.

The flowers looked good against the glossy blackness of her hair; it was pleasant to watch her as it had been pleasant to listen to the noise she made. Then, as though conscious of his gaze, she looked in his direction. For a moment she smiled, and started to call something, but her face changed almost immediately. Fear came into it, and she scrambled to her feet. Dom realized she was going to run away and was determined to stop her, so he shouted and ran round the side of the pool. She did not look back but ran off into the wood.

He chased her, trying to ignore the pain and weakness in his leg. He saw the brown slimness of her figure ahead of him, lost and then glimpsed again among the green. He shouted a second time, commanding her to stop and telling her he would beat her if she did not. It was the sort of shout the hunters used to the women of the tribe when they did something wrong, and it always caused them to cower in submission. But the girl ran on, and he felt she was outdistancing him. Trying to run faster, he put his foot into a hole, stumbled and fell. His head cracked against the low branch of a tree; he dropped and lay still.

Soft fingers touched him gently; a hand was cool against his brow. Dom opened his eyes and saw the girl very close, kneeling beside him and bending over him. But he was too weak to move, almost too weak to speak. Even when he saw the sharply pointed stone in her hand, he could do nothing. She would kill him now, he thought, and the shame of it troubled him more than the idea of death—a hunter, to be killed by a girl . . .

Yet she did not drive the stone into his throat or breast as he expected. Instead she used it to slash at the wound in his leg. The pain was wrenchingly sharp, and took away his senses again.

When they returned she was still there, sitting and watching him. There was something on his leg—he looked at it and saw that the wound was covered by a small mound of leaves, bound round and held in place by plaited grasses. He plucked at it with his fingers and the girl spoke to him.

He had no idea what the words meant but the tone was chiding. She put her hand over his and pulled it away. He realized that the pressure of the leaves against his flesh was soothing, and that the wound itself was throbbing less than before.

She said more words that he did not know. She had a small plant in her hand and she put this close to his face. Dom looked at her, shaking his head. Then she broke off a leaf from the plant, put it in her mouth, and chewed it. He understood that she was showing him it was good to eat, and when she offered him the plant a second time he broke off a leaf and chewed it as she had done. The taste was sour, and he spat it out. Again her tone rebuked him; she pointed to the plant and to his leg and nodded her head vigorously. She pushed another leaf toward his mouth and, as much out of weakness as anything, he let his lips open to take it. It still tasted sour but it was not really unpleasant. He chewed the leaf, and the girl smiled and nodded her approval.

She stayed with him all day. Later she brought him fruit and berries to eat, and water in a big leaf. Dom drowsed between sleeping and waking. Once he managed to get up and tried to walk, but he was very weak and it hurt too much. The girl shook her head and gently helped him lie down again.

During the afternoon she left him for a time, and returned with her arms full of leaves and springy moss. She made a bed for him to lie on, in a hollow between two trees, and then, sitting by him, made a covering, weaving grass and leaves and moss together into a kind of blanket. Dom watched her, astonished by the skill of her moving fingers.

She brought him more fruit and berries before the sun went down. Then she said something in her strange language, smiled and went away. Dom called after her; she turned and smiled again but did not come back. She went away through the trees and was lost to his view.

He awoke during the night. He was aware of being alone, for the first time in his life not hearing the breathing sounds of the sleeping tribe around him. And the girl had gone. She had helped him, but it made no difference. He was alone, away from the tribe, and certain to die.

Then he slept again.

4

VA SLIPPED INTO THE VILLAGE THROUGH THE
gap in the hedge just as the cattle were being
brought in. She went to her mother's hut and
was greeted by her lovingly; they embraced and
kissed each other as they always did when they met,
however brief the separation had been.

Her mother asked her: "Have you been to your
wood, Va?"

Va nodded. "Yes."

She had told her mother, and the Village Mother,
about the wood, but no one else. It was her secret—
the wood itself, the pool where she bathed, the

animals that had learned to come and feed from her hands. None of the other girls in the village had such a secret, because none of them liked to slip away on their own as she did. But she, as she knew, was a special person, the only granddaughter of the Village Mother whose wisdom guided the life and destiny of all their people.

She thought of telling her mother about the boy she had found, or who, rather, had found her— of how she had run away when he chased her, and then he had fallen and lain still and she had gone back to find him unconscious, and afterward had tended him.

She almost did tell her but at the last moment drew back from it. Because she realized that if she told her that she would have to tell her something else also—that the boy had carried a club of bone. This meant, as she had known when she first saw him standing by the pool, watching her, that he belonged to the savages, those men who had slaughtered the grazing cattle and afterward attacked the village. And for that the Village Mother had pronounced doom on them.

Once such a thing was told it must be told to the

Village Mother also, and Va guessed the order that would be given once she heard of the wounded boy in the wood. There would still be time to send men with knives to kill him, before the rest of the savages returned.

So Va did not speak about the boy. That night, before she went to sleep, she thought of him, alone and ill under the trees. She had lanced his wound and put healing herbs on it to draw out the poison, and given him leaves to chew from the plant that was a remedy for fevers, but he still might die. The edges of the wound had been red and ugly, the skin swollen all round, and his head burningly hot to her touch.

It might be better, after all, if he did die. Because there could be no doubt that he was one of the savages—the club, which he had insisted on keeping by him even while she tended him, was proof enough. She remembered the way he had run after her, the great club swinging as he pursued her. Once he was strong again he would be as evil and murderous as the others.

She had not spoken to her mother about him because she could not bear the thought of being the cause of the death of someone whom, less than an hour before, she had been nursing. She realized, though, that she had been wrong in keeping silent. The Village Mother had pronounced doom on the savages, and so what she had done amounted to defiance and disobedience. She shivered, not from fear but from shame at her own disloyalty. In the morning she would tell.

But when the morning came she still could not bring herself to do so. And it might not be necessary, she told herself: the boy might have died in the night. She left the village as soon as the opening was made in the hedge and made her way along the valley to the wood. As she drew near the spot where she had left him she felt a sudden fear, remembering how wild and fierce he had looked when he was chasing her. She went cautiously and warily through the trees, alert for a lurking figure. Then she saw him lying in the bed she had made for him, and guessed that he was dead.

Fear turned to sorrow; then to pleasure as, kneeling to look at him, she saw his eyes open. They stared at each other. His face was different from the faces of the boys and men she knew—darker, heavier, more powerful. Fiercer, too, she thought, with a small shudder of apprehension. But the features changed as he recognized her—not quite into a smile but at least into a look of welcome and greeting.

Va said: "Let me see your wound."

He frowned in bewilderment but nodded when she pointed to his leg. She stripped away the bandage of leaves and examined it. The wound was still ugly and inflamed, but the flesh surrounding it was less swollen. She felt his forehead and found it cooler.

"You are getting better," she said, "but I will put more herbs on to make sure."

He said something as meaningless to her as her words had been to him. She went away to find the herbs she needed, and fresh leaves to hold them in place. When she came back he was sitting up, looking for her. She smiled, and saw his lips move slightly in response.

Sitting beside him she plaited grass into a cord to bind the dressing. As she did so, not thinking, she began singing softly. The boy said something in his strange language and she stopped. He shook his head and spoke again, asking for something but she did not know what.

"What is the matter?" she asked. "Are you hungry? Thirsty? I will get you water and find berries for you as soon as I have seen to your wound."

He spoke more and Va shook her head. Then he made even weirder noises. At first she thought he was in pain—they were more like howls of agony than anything else. Then she realized what he was doing and burst out laughing: he was trying to imitate her singing!

He said other words, and she realized that he wanted her to sing for him. She laughed again, and did so. The song was one that mothers sang to their babies, gentle and low. She could see from his face that he liked it, and was pleased.

Until she remembered who he was, and the doom the Village Mother had pronounced on all the savages. The song died on her lips. He looked at her and said something urgently, clearly asking her to go on. What she ought to do, in obedience to the Village Mother, was to run back to the village and tell them, so that the men could come with spears to kill him. But thinking of that she knew she could not do it. It did not matter that he was a savage, did not matter that he had chased her and threatened her with his club. What mattered was that she had found him helpless and had nursed him, that she had saved him from the poison that otherwise would have taken his life. She could not let him die.

Knowing this she took up the song again, and the boy listened to her, his face not fierce but peaceful. Va finished making the cord, and bandaged up his wound. It was a good song for him, she thought. He was something like a baby—in his present helplessness, at least.

Va brought fruit and berries and water, and watched him while he ate and drank. Squatting near him, she asked:

"What is your name?"

He stared at her but made no answer.

"My name is Va." She touched her breast lightly with her hand. "Va."

"Va. . . ."

It came strangely from his lips, the syllable thick and heavy, making her name sound quite different from any other time she had heard it. She pointed to him.

"What is your name?" He shook his head. "I am Va—who are you?"

She pointed to herself when she said "Va," then to him. He understood, and said:

"Dom."

She smiled and said the name herself. "Dom. . . ." She liked the sound of it.

They played a game of naming: trees, bushes, the sky, water, the parts of the body. Sometimes they failed to understand each other, even with many repetitions, and many of the words she quickly forgot; but it was pleasant to play the game, to have their minds make fleeting contact across the barrier of their alien languages.

Eventually Dom struggled to his feet. Va offered to help him but he showed her he could manage on his own. He used his club to assist himself, and swung it from his hand when he was upright. Va looked at it with loathing, but if he noticed that he did not pay attention. He hobbled in the direction of the pool and she followed him.

At the edge of the pool there was more naming: the pool itself, water—she bent down and cupped some in her hands to show him—a bird that flew away from its perch on a rock at the far side. Then Dom made funny motions with his arms. It took her some time to realize that he was mimicking the motions of swimming. She told him what the word was but that did not satisfy him; he pointed first to her and then to the pool.

He wanted to see her swim. Va smiled and nodded and, throwing off her dress, stepped into the water. She swam about in the pool for a time and then beckoned to him to join her. He shook his head. His leg, of course, would prevent him swimming—he could only just walk on it.

She got out of the pool and found him fingering the material of her dress, examining it curiously. He himself wore a short tunic made of animal skin, antelope she guessed. Her own people wore skins in the cold weather, but the dress had been made by weaving fibers from the stems of the blue-flowered plants that grew higher up the valley. His people almost certainly lacked such skills; they were, after all, savages, as the Village Mother had said. . . . Va recalled her disobedience, and quickly put the thought away.

She took the dress from him and put it on. He

picked up her belt from the ground and looked at the stone knife she kept in it. He fingered this as he had fingered the dress, trying the point against the flesh of his arm. Perhaps they did not have stone knives, either; did not have anything but the clubs and daggers taken from the skeletons of dead animals.

She drew the knife from her belt and put it in his hand. She said:

"You can keep it, Dom."

He stared at her, not understanding.

"Keep it," she said. "We have lots of knives in the village."

He was still puzzled. Va closed his hand over it with her own, then pushed the hand away. He understood at last and nodded, smiling.

So the day passed. They played the naming game, and Va found fruit and berries for them both; at times they simply sat together by the pool, or Va sang for him. In late afternoon, before she went away, she dressed his wound again. It was much cleaner and healthier in appearance. He still walked with difficulty but most of the poison had been drawn out: she was sure he would get better. She pointed to the sky, where the sun was sinking behind the leafy branches of the trees, and then in the direction of the village. He understood and watched her go, leaning on his great club.

This time there could be no question of Va telling her mother what had happened; she had made up her mind to protect Dom even from her own people. Next morning, impatient, she set out as soon as the hedge was opened and the scouts had gone to keep watch against the possibility of the savages returning early. She saw one of them as she made her way toward the wood—a boy not much older than herself called Gri. He wanted her to stay and talk to him, but she would not. She liked him well enough but now she thought how soft and weak his face was compared with Dom's.

The moss-bed was empty when she got there. She wondered if Dom had gone away, back to his savage people, and was sad. She called and got no answer except from the birds. She went then to the pool and sat on a flat rock that overhung the water. The sun was shining but here under the trees it was dark, with a gloom that matched her mood.

There was a flash of movement along the branch

of one of the trees that fringed the pool. She knew what it was: one of the squirrels which in the past had learned to come and take nuts from her hand. They had not come near yesterday because Dom had been with her, but they knew she was alone again.

The squirrel raced down the trunk of the tree and along the ground to where she sat. It perched on its haunches and looked up at her comically. Va showed her empty hands, but it still stared at her with its black beads of eyes. She said:

"I will find you some nuts, squirrel. But not yet. There is all day to find nuts for you."

As though it had understood her words, the squirrel whisked away and darted back up into the tree. Va looked down into the pool. A shaft of sunlight struck between the branches and turned the water on the far side to gold. Nearer it was dark and limpid, and bending over she could see her own face reflected. She stared at it, wondering how it looked to other people, how it had looked to Dom. She wondered if he would remember her.

She watched the shadowy image of herself, her mind sad and quiet. Suddenly something else came into the reflection—the dark outline of a figure standing behind and above her. She whirled in quick fear and then, her heart still beating tumultuously, laughed for joy. It was Dom who stood behind her.

She was astonished that he had managed to creep up so quietly that she had not been aware of his approach. None of the boys from the village could have done that; however preoccupied she had been she would have heard something. As the squirrel had done . . . that was why it had scurried back into the tree.

Dom smiled. He was carrying something and he offered it to her. He had made a score or more of flowers—bright pointed stars of scarlet—into a kind of necklace, threading each one through the stem of the next. It was clumsily done but Va smiled her approval.

"It is very pretty, Dom."

He took the chain of flowers and put it over her head, around her neck. He spoke words that she did not understand. She smiled again.

"We will go and find fruit to eat. And perhaps find nuts for my squirrel."

She put her hand in his and together they went away from the pool. He limped a little, but she could tell his leg was almost well.

· · ·

They found fruit and berries and ate them as they walked; Va also gathered some nuts and put them in the small pouch she carried on her belt. Wandering with no particular aim they came back in due course to the pool, and Dom made the swimming motions with his arms to show that he wanted to see her go in. So she slipped into the pool and swam from the shadowed dark to the golden sunlit water. Looking back to where Dom stood—seeing him only hazily from the sunlight that dazzled her eyes—she called him to come and swim with her: his leg was well enough for that. He made no move, though. Probably because he did not understand, she thought, and swam back to the bank. She told him again to come in, but he only stood there, looking down at her.

After a while he stooped and stretched out his hand toward her. She guessed he was offering to help her get out of the pool. She clasped her hand in his and then, laughing, pulled hard. Dom struggled for a moment to keep his balance before tumbling forward.

Their hands unlinked as he fell with a great splash beside her. Still laughing, Va swam round him, trod water and splashed at him. Dom was making clumsy threshing movements with his arms and legs, gasping and spluttering and swallowing water. When his head disappeared below the surface she realized what it was that had kept him from coming in when she called to him. It was nothing to do with his leg being hurt: swimming was another art that was unknown to the savages.

The water was deep in that part of the pool but shallower farther along. Va dived under, fishing for him. She got hold of his arm—he resisted but she managed to pull him along. Where the pool's bottom shelved, she let him go. He went on threshing frantically until he realized that she was standing upright in the water, and stood up, gasping, beside her.

Va's laughter stopped at the sight of his face. He was frightened, and also angry. He waded through the water toward her, his arm raised to strike. The blow landed harmlessly on her shoulder as she dodged and, plunging back into the water, swam out into the center of the pool. He shouted angrily but could not follow her. ·

It was her turn to be frightened: for the moment

she was safe in the pool but she could not stay there. She saw Dom scramble up the bank and take hold of the club which he had dropped when he offered her his hand. He was a savage after all; as soon as she left the pool he would strike her with it and kill her.

But after a moment or two his face and voice softened. He made a beckoning gesture, but Va shook her head violently. He was only trying to persuade her to come out so he could kill her. Even when he dropped the club and beckoned again, with both arms this time, she made the same response.

Then he did a strange thing. Leaving the club behind him on the ground, he dropped awkwardly into the pool. She thought he was coming after her and, although she was already in deep water, swam farther out. He called to her, and waded out until the water was up to his chest. When she refused to come he waded still farther, though it was plain from the expression on his face that the depth of the water dismayed him. At last he stood with water up to his neck, his hands helplessly raised.

He was showing her that his anger was at an end. When Va finally smiled, he smiled in return. She swam to him and he took her arm, but not roughly.

He said something she did not understand, and she told him that what she had done had been intended as a joke—that she had not wanted to hurt him or frighten him. It was his turn not to understand, but they laughed together.

They played for an hour or so in the pool, and Va tried to teach him to swim. It was not easy: he kept spluttering and sinking and a couple of times she had to pull him back into shallow water. At last, though, he managed a kind of swimming, for half a dozen strokes at a time.

Va said: "In a few days you will be swimming as well as I do, Dom."

He did not know what the words meant, but he smiled and nodded.

Afterward they lay on the grassy bank, where the patch of sunlight had now settled. They ate the rest of the fruit they had gathered and rested from their exertions in the water. The sun moved on across the sky until it was time for Va to be going back to the village. She said so to Dom, who smiled and nodded uncomprehendingly. So she pointed toward the sun and then in the direction of the village as she had done the day before, to explain that she must go.

Dom shook his head, more emphatically when she repeated the gestures. He did not want her to leave, and for her part she did not want to go. She thought of the possibility of the two of them staying on together here. She knew where to find food; they had the pool to swim in, the animals to play with, each other for company. In due course the rest of the savages would grow tired of trying to get into the village and go somewhere else. When that happened she could take Dom back to the village with her. By that time he would no longer be a savage because she would have taught him things, as she had already taught him to swim. The Village Mother would not order him to be killed then: she would accept him as one of their people.

She had lain back in the sun, thinking of this, imagining how it all might be. Looking idly up into the tree she saw her squirrel again. She clutched Dom's arm, pointing to it. They both stayed very still and the squirrel came down the tree trunk onto the ground. Va still had the nuts she had gathered in her pouch; she took one out and held it in her hand.

The squirrel ran across to take it from her. Dom

did not move until it was a few feet away; then, before she realized what was happening, he swung the club of bone through the air in a flashing arc. It hit the squirrel's head and crushed it.

Va cried out in distress. Dom picked up the squirrel's corpse and held it in front of her for inspection. He was smiling, proud of the skill with which he had swung his club and killed this small animal. A trickle of blood ran from its mouth.

She shouted at him: "You are a savage! You know of nothing except killing. I hate you for coming into my wood and killing my squirrel!"

Dom looked at her, puzzled but still smiling. She scrambled to her feet and ran away from him through the trees. He called, and then ran after her. She heard the thud of his feet, but the sound fell farther and farther behind. His leg was still not strong enough for him to be able to keep up with her.

She was clear of him before she reached the outskirts of the wood, but still ran on. She met Gri, not at the place where she had seen him in the morning but close to the village. He said:

"You are just in time, Va. The savages are coming back. I saw them far up the valley."

. . .

As soon as she got back, Va went to see the Village Mother. She ruled and looked after all the people, but because she was the mother of Va's mother Va was special to her. She had long white hair, a kind strong face, and was wiser, Va knew, than anyone in the world.

She told her the story of finding Dom and helping him. She admitted that she had been wrong in not telling the Village Mother about it at the beginning, and begged her forgiveness.

When she had finished, the Village Mother said:

"Your fault was one of kindness in the first place. That is better than other faults, but a fault is still a fault. These people are savages, as I have said. They have no arts, no skills except in hunting and killing. They seek to destroy us, and will do so if they can. You thought you could teach this boy, and some things perhaps you could. He could learn swimming. Perhaps he could understand the beauty of flowers and the joy of singing. But there are more important things he could never be taught; and things he knows which he cannot unlearn. So he killed the squirrel, a pretty, harmless creature, because killing lies deep in his nature."

Va listened and wept. The Village Mother put a hand on her head.

"You are sad, daughter. It is right you should be, as punishment for your disobedience. But the sadness will not last. Soon the savages will tire of trying to get into our village and go away. Then you will forget this boy."

Before sunset the savages were outside the hedge, raucously shouting their hatred. Va listened with horror to the ugly sound. At times she thought she could hear Dom's voice among the rest.

5

DOM WAS MORE CONFUSED THAN ANYTHING
else when Va ran away. He did not really
become angry until she was completely lost to
view, and he realized he could not hope to catch her.
He went on, limping, to the edge of the wood and
saw her far off, a small dot in the distance. He
watched until she disappeared into a copse and then,
both furious and miserable, retraced his steps.

The body of the squirrel was lying by the pool
and he picked it up and looked at it. The single
stroke with which he had crushed its skull had been
a good one—something to set against her prowess

in swimming. The fact that instead of praising him she had run away made no sense. He stared at the squirrel in disgust: it was not even good eating. He tossed it into the undergrowth and gloomily stared at the pool.

He had liked this place better than any he had ever seen. The green hush tempered by bird song, the dimness broken here and there by spears of sunlight, the animals and bright flowers and whispering water: it was as though his eyes and ears had been suddenly opened so that for the first time he could truly see and hear. Va had shown these things to him. Now, with her gone, although the other things remained he was only conscious of what was absent. Without her it meant nothing.

So he turned his back on the pool and left the wood. He went in the direction of the village but traveled warily; he knew what would happen to him if, by himself, he were to fall in with the men of Va's tribe. He saw no sign of them, though, and when he reached the open space in which the village stood, he noticed that the gap in the hedge was closed and the villagers and their cattle were safe inside. Not long after that he heard the sounds of his own tribe approaching. They came noisily: they were not on a hunt and they wanted it known that this land was theirs. The triumphant shouts of the hunters went ahead of them.

They stopped, staring, when they saw Dom. His father came forward from the rest. He stood before Dom and put his hands on his shoulders, shaking him to make sure he was not a ghost.

He said: "We thought you were dead, my son. We returned to where we had left you and you were not there. We guessed you had crawled into a ditch to die. The old woman said that the evil spirit was so strong in you that you could not live another day."

Dom showed his leg with the wound healing, and flexed it to show how much strength had already come back.

"I was given help."

"What help?"

His father stood back from him, suspiciously. It was plain he thought the evil spirit might still be in Dom's mind, twisting his thoughts. He said:

"No one of the tribe was with you."

"Not from the tribe," Dom said. "It was a girl, from that place there."

He pointed to the village, and told the story. At the end his father said:

"You say that when you killed a squirrel she ran away from you. So the evil spirits were at work in her mind also."

"She helped me. I am better because of the help she gave me."

His father nodded. "This proves her madness. She knew you to be an enemy: she should have killed you when you were helpless, not helped you. Perhaps they are all mad in that place. It makes no difference. Mad or not, we will destroy them."

His anger swelled up again as he remembered how they had defied him. He led the hunters forward into the clearing and they shouted with rage. Dom went with them and did his best to shout with the rest; but he kept thinking of Va and the wood. He knew that what his father said was right—he was the chief and therefore always right—but he could not help remembering the coolness of the pool and how good it had been to walk with Va in the shade of the trees.

Yet she had run away from him, for no reason, and refused to stop when he called her. Dom's own anger was stirred by the recollection of that. In the end he shouted as loudly as the other hunters.

"We will kill you! This land is ours—we are the masters of it. Come out and fight if you are not women. And if you do not come out, then we will come and kill you where you hide!"

They went up close to the hedge in their frenzy, but a shower of stones drove them away.

That night they ate the meat which they had brought back from the day's hunt. It was the first meat Dom had eaten since the tribe left him. He remembered the fruits and berries Va had brought, but thought how much better this meat was, full of red blood to give a hunter strength. From meat also one acquired that which was best in the spirit of the animal: courage from the lion, cunning from the pig, fleetness of foot from the antelope. What use were fruit and berries compared to this?

When they sat with full bellies, Dom's father pointed to his belt.

"What is that?"

Dom explained that it was the stone knife the girl had given him. His father put out his hand and

Dom handed the knife to him. He examined it carefully.

"It is much better than the knives our women make from the jaws of antelope. Why did she give you such a thing?" He tried it on the antelope hide he was wearing. "It cuts well."

He put the knife away in his own belt. It was something Dom had expected and he did not resent it. Everything the tribe possessed belonged to the chief.

"There will be many things to take from them," his father said. "Not only their beasts."

One of the hunters said: "But we cannot get into the place. We have been many days in this valley, and we still cannot bring them to battle."

"We will destroy them all," Dom's father said, "and take their goods. There are the tree-caves also. When we have slain them we will have those caves as shelter against the rains."

The same hunter asked: "But how will we get through the hedge of thorns to be able to slay them?"

He was a powerful man, as strong as that one who had challenged Dom's father following the defeat on the hillside, and who had been killed by him.

Dom's father said: "We will stay here until we find a way."

He looked at the hunter with fierce eyes, and the hunter dropped his head, Dom's father said:

"They come out during the day while we are away hunting. Dom saw this: it was not the evil spirit telling lies to his mind. He met the girl, who tended his wound." He patted the stone knife in his belt. "Here is proof of it. They wait until we have gone and then bring their beasts out to graze. They watch for us coming back, cowards that they are, and run when they see us. So we will not go away, but wait. They may stay in there many days, but in the end they must come out."

"If we must wait many days," another hunter said, "we will have no meat. There is no game left in this part of the valley. We must go far away to hunt."

"Then some will wait," Dom's father said, "while others hunt. And to make the meat last longer the women will cut it into strips and dry it in the sun, as they did when we lived in the grasslands. Fresh meat is good, but it will be better to have their beasts and stone knives, and their tree-caves."

He looked hard at the other hunters, who listened to him in silence.

So next day the tribe stayed close by the village. Nothing happened except that the hunters went as near to the fence as they dared and hurled jeers and threats at those inside. No gap was opened in the hedge, and no one came out.

On the second day half the hunters went away down the valley to look for game, while the rest, along with the women and some of the boys and the old ones, kept watch on the clearing. Dom was one of the ones who stayed—his leg was not yet strong enough for the chase—but his father was with the hunters who went away. His strength and cunning would be the more needed in the hunt because their numbers were fewer.

That evening they returned with their kill, and the day after the women cut up the remaining meat into strips and dried it. On the fourth day they had dried meat to chew and some of the hunters grumbled, but stopped their grumbling when Dom's father looked at them.

By the sixth day even the dried meat was almost finished, and half the hunters went off again, leaving the rest behind. Dom's leg was now quite well but his father ordered him to stay, and although like the other hunters he was bored and restless he was bound to obey. The hours crawled by. Then in the middle of the afternoon someone noticed that branches of thorn were being pulled away to make a gap in the hedge.

The hunters started to run forward as soon as they saw what was happening; and at the same time men were coming out of the village. These formed a line and hurled stones at the hunters as they rushed toward them. A couple fell wounded; then the two bands came to grips, one side swinging their clubs of bone and the others using their stone knives.

More and more men came out of the village and joined in the battle. Dom cracked one with his club and saw him fall, but at that instant another was on him from the side, and he felt the sharp pain of the knife piercing his arm. He struggled to swing the club again, but the man dodged the blow. He saw one of the hunters go down with a knife in his back, and another from a knife struck hard under his ribs.

The men from the village seemed to be everywhere, and he had to fight desperately to keep them off.

Then suddenly he realized that the hunters were running away, and found himself running with them. The enemy pursued them as far as the edge of the clearing, and their cries of triumph and derision followed the hunters for a long way after that.

They gathered together in another clearing farther up the valley. The defeat had shocked them, and they were wordless and miserable. Dom knew why they had been beaten. It was not just that, with half their men away in the hunt, they had been outnumbered three to one, or more. What had really made the difference was that Dom's father, their chief, had not been there. They had had no one to rally them when the villagers came out and attacked them; it was because of that they had run like monkeys, not fought like men.

The chief's fury was enormous when he came back with the other hunters. He strode among the ones who had been left behind, striking them as they cowered from his rage and calling them women—worse than women since they had allowed men who were themselves no better than women to drive them away. They took the blows and the insults, but then they too turned angry and sullen. That hunter who had protested before said:

"This place is no good for us. The lands in the south are as good as these, and there is much game. There we can eat fresh meat every day."

Dom's father went fiercely toward him, but there were murmurs from other hunters as well. Dom knew what they were thinking. It had been the chief's idea to split the hunters into two bands. He had gone away, and that was why the villagers had beaten them.

"We will have fresh meat every day," Dom's father said, "when we have killed the enemy. And we will have their tree-caves and their stone knives, and everything else."

Someone said: "When is when? The days go by and nothing happens."

Another spoke. "You said you would find us a cave in the hills. If we had that we would not need their tree-caves. And we can do without their stone knives. The knives our women make are good enough."

It was not just one—all the hunters were grumbling. Dom remembered a tale the old women told of a chief, long ago, who had failed in his duty to the tribe, and how the rest of the hunters had turned on him together and killed him. A thing that had happened once could happen again. With his heart pounding he looked at his father, and saw that he knew this too.

His father turned from the hunter who had first spoken, and stood in front of another, whose face was bloody from the fight in the clearing. Speaking only to him, he said:

"You are a coward. You ran from men who are as weak as women."

The hunter looked at him, daring to reply.

"I remember that you ran, too, on the hillside."

Dom's father smashed him to the ground with his fist. He shouted:

"We ran then because the stones of the hillside came down on us! Not as cowards who run from cowards."

He had chosen that one man in the hope that by striking him down he could intimidate the rest. But this time the other hunters did not stay silent in fear. It was another who shouted back:

"Where is the cave you promised us? And why were you not here to fight, you who call us cowards?"

Their grumbling had turned into a low growl that rose almost to a roar. In a moment they would attack their chief all together, and strong as he was he must die quickly. Dom cried out:

"I know a way of getting through the hedge. . . ."

The grumbling stopped at his words. His father stared at him. One of the hunters laughed.

"Another evil spirit has got into him through the cut in his arm. Or perhaps the old one is still there. The boy is mad."

His father said: "Speak, if you have anything to say."

Dom said: "You said that the stones came down on us from the hillside that day. That was true. And the enemy's place lies under the hill. When we went up there and looked down at them I saw a big stone, as tall as a man and as wide as four men side by side. If we could roll that down the slope it would break through the hedge, and we could run in after it."

The hunter who had laughed said scornfully:

"I also remember that stone. It is fixed in the earth. You could not roll it down."

Dom said: "But if we scratched away the earth in front of it, maybe it would roll."

There was a silence; then Dom's father said:

"We will look at this stone. Come."

He turned and walked away. Dom followed him and so, after a moment's hesitation, did the other hunters.

The stone was bigger than Dom had thought, covered with moss and lichen and with small plants growing in crevices where earth had gathered. It seemed impossible that it could be moved, and he half expected his father to say so, and cuff him for his foolishness. But his father went very carefully all round the stone, examining it. After that he stared down the slope toward the village.

"If it could be made to roll down it would break through the hedge, as the boy said. If it can be moved." He looked at the hunters. "We will dig the earth away and find out."

He had won back his ascendancy over them, for the time being at least. At his command they set to work, scrabbling at the earth with their hands, loosening the soil and pulling it away. They could not all get in under the stone together so Dom's father made them work in relays: he did not dig himself, of course, because he was the chief.

They worked hard and for a long time, sweating in the rays from the sun which, though slanting now across the valley, were still hot. Only when the sun had dipped below the facing hill did the chief permit them to stop.

Dom looked at the hole they had made; it seemed very small compared with the size of the boulder. With the other hunters he put his hands against the rough surface of the stone, trying to move it. Nothing happened.

"We will come here tomorrow," Dom's father said, "and dig again."

In the morning the cut in his arm was sore and inflamed, and Dom wondered if the evil spirit really had returned to him. He would have liked to go and search for the plant which Va had put on the wound in his leg, but his father commanded all the hunters to go up again to the stone on the hillside, and Dom had to go with them.

The sky was light but the sun had not yet risen

above the hill; there was a glow of gold in the blue sky behind its crest. But one could see very clearly, and he looked down beyond the hedge into the village. Animals were there: cattle in their pen and hens pecking the earth. None of the people could be seen; doubtless they were still sleeping in their tree-caves. He wondered in which cave Va was; then his father saw him standing idle and ordered him to dig.

The sun came up and they sweated again. Down in the village people came out of their huts. They looked up at the hunters and mocked them as they had done the previous day. Dom saw women and girls there as well as men and, once more filled with anger at the thought of her running away from him, tried to pick Va out. But the distance was too great to see if she were there; the enemy's jeers came thinly through the air.

They dug round the sides and back of the stone as well as under the front. The work was hard, and although the hunters' hands were tough and calloused, they grew sore. Some said it was time to try pushing the stone again, and in the end Dom's father agreed. They put their shoulders to it, striving to make it move, but with no success.

There was grumbling among them. Dom's father shouted:

"Push! Push hard!"

He came and heaved against the stone himself, elbowing a hunter out of the way to do so. Then they all felt it, a tiny rocking, almost imperceptible. They heaved again and it rocked a little more. Dom's father said:

"It is beginning to come loose. Now dig!"

They dug and heaved and dug again. Each time they tried it moved more positively—after another hour or two they could rock it to and fro. Wiping sweat from his eyes, feeling the soreness and smart of his wounded arm, Dom looked briefly down into the village. He thought of Va with anger and a savage joy. Soon he and the other hunters would be in there, and he would show her what it meant not to obey his commands.

On the next attempt the stone almost came out of its socket in the earth. The hunters went back to their digging with a will, because now they could all see the prospect of success, of fighting and triumph. They dug and pushed, dug and pushed.

Then, pushing, Dom heard his father's cry of exultation close by him and, putting all his strength against the stone, felt it lurch forward, tilting up and away, out of the earth which had held it.

They all shouted together as the stone rolled down the slope, but their shouts died when its progress halted after no more than a yard or two. The hunters stared at it, discouraged.

"It has moved once," Dom's father said, "so it will move again. Push!"

It moved but stopped after a few more feet. Unless they could get it to roll fast it would be useless as a means of breaking through the hedge. Near the village the slope was much less steep, almost level. No amount of straining, Dom realized, would enable them to move it down there.

The hunters heaved and struggled. Dom felt the sting of his wound as his arm pressed against the jagged surface, but ignored it. The stone rolled again, and this time went on rolling. They saw it gathering speed as it bumped on down the slope, rocking and scattering smaller stones that lay in its path. Shouting, the hunters ran after it.

The men of the village came running as the

boulder careered downhill toward the hedge. Dom heard their cries of amazement and dismay, mingling with the hunters' shouts of excitement. Bouncing in a cloud of dust, the stone reached the more gentle slope at the bottom and without checking, rolled on. It hit the hedge and smashed through it, making a gap several feet across and crushing some of the village men who stood inside. Before it finally came to rest it had crashed into one of the tree-caves and split it open.

The battle was not a long one, but it was bloody enough. The men of the village, in among their homes, fought much harder than they had done on the first encounter; but the hunters fought better than on the second. They were at full strength, they were relishing the triumph of having forced their way through the barrier which had held them at bay for so long, and they were led by their great chief, Dom's father, swinging his huge club of bone. Nothing could stand in their way now.

Dom, forgetting wound and weariness, forgetting everything except the ecstasy of battle, wielded his club with the rest. Very soon its whiteness was stained with the blood of the enemy. Like the other hunters he killed mercilessly, giving no quarter. Within fifteen minutes it was over, and the earth littered with dead or dying men, among whom the hunters walked, shouting their victory.

The women and children of the village huddled together in shocked and weeping groups. As soon as his mind cooled from its fever of killing, Dom looked for Va among them. He found her quite soon, clinging to an older woman. With the bloody club in his hand, he said:

"Come!"

She stared at him, shivering with fear, her face stained with tears. Despite his anger he found it good to see her again. He would beat her for running away, as he must, but perhaps he would not beat her very hard. Then they would go to the wood together, and bathe in the pool, and find fruit to eat. He would make another necklace of scarlet blossoms and put it round her neck.

When she did not move, he said more harshly:

"Come. We have conquered your people. From now on you will do as I say."

She still cowered away. Dom passed the club into

his left hand and roughly grabbed her arm with his right. She moaned, and the older woman cried out, but he pulled her toward him.

As he did so he heard his father's voice calling. He turned and his father came to him. Dom said:

"This is the girl who helped me, and then ran away."

Dom's father looked at Va. "She is of an age for mating."

"Yes," Dom said. "I will take her for my mate. But first I will beat her for running away."

His father laughed. "She is of an age for mating, but you are not, boy! I will take this one."

"No." Dom looked up at his father. "You cannot do that. She is mine."

"Cannot?"

His father stared at him, more curious than angry, still good-humored from the victory he had won. He grinned.

"Run away, boy. Leave the girl to me."

"No!" Dom was frightened, but desperate. "I will not."

He pulled at Va's arm again, trying to convey to her that they must both run now, to get away from his father. But she moaned again, and held back. Then Dom's father roared as curiosity and amusement gave way to rage. His heavy fist smashed at Dom. Dom dodged the first blow, but the second knocked him senseless.

6

THE NIGHT AFTER SHE HAD RUN AWAY FROM
Dom, Va could not sleep. She lay awake, thinking of what had happened and sobbing from
time to time. It was her punishment, as the Village
Mother had said, and she must endure the unhappi-
ness. It would not last. The savages would go away
in due course, and after that she would forget about
Dom. She would marry someone, Gri perhaps, and
live her life in the village as her people had always
done. At last, when she was old and wise, she would
be the Village Mother like her grandmother.

But as the slow hours passed, she thought less of

the Village Mother's words and more of Dom. She thought of the way he had learned to smile during the two days they had spent together. She remembered his anger when she had pulled him down into the pool, and then how he had laughed afterward.

It was true that he had killed the squirrel, and grinned as he held out the small corpse to show her. But he had not known that he was doing anything wrong—to him her tame squirrel had been just another animal to slaughter. Because he was one of the savages, the Village Mother had said, and of course that was true. She had also said that a savage could never change, would always be a cruel and hateful killer.

Was that true, too? Although she knew the Village Mother was wiser than anyone else, Va could not bring herself to believe it. She thought of that morning of the second day, when she had found the moss-bed empty and gone down unhappily to the pool—of how good it had been when she had realized that the face reflected in the pool beside her own was Dom's. And how he had brought her the necklace of flowers. That was not the way a savage acted. There were other things in his mind besides the lust for killing.

She made her mind up as light was beginning to filter into the hut, in promise of the new dawn. She would go to the wood again, as soon as the gap was opened in the hedge. Perhaps Dom would still be there, waiting for her. She would teach him—not just things like swimming but how to love small animals, not kill them. The Village Mother was wrong because she did not know Dom. All she knew was that the savages had killed men and cattle, and tried to break into the village. She had not seen Dom's face when he offered her the necklace of flowers, nor when they laughed together in the pool. Her own first thought had been right: he could be taught not to be a savage. She could teach him.

But the gap was not opened in the hedge that morning because this time the savages did not go away. They stayed in the clearing, occasionally coming up close to the hedge and shouting until they were driven off with stones. Va looked for Dom but did not see him. Only the men were allowed to climb up on the huts to throw stones; she had to peer out dimly through the thorns.

The fact that she had not seen him did not mean that he was not there; but just as the previous evening she had imagined she heard his voice crying hatred with the rest, so now she felt sure in her heart that he had not returned to his savage tribe—that he was still in the wood, waiting for her to come back. Tomorrow, perhaps, she would be able to do so. But next day the savages were still there; and the day after the same.

That night the Village Mother spoke to them, assembled together near the fire.

"They are more cunning than I thought," she said, "and more persistent. They know we have been grazing the cattle while they were away hunting. Therefore they stay here to prevent your doing this."

One of the men said: "What should we do, Mother? We have fodder for only a few days. Soon the cattle will be starving. Should we not go out and fight them?"

"They are stronger than you are," the Village Mother said, "and more skilled at fighting. One expects as much of savages. It would be folly to attack them; they would only defeat you as they did before."

Another man said: "They have shamed us, Mother. We must not skulk here and watch our women and children starve. It is better to be killed than do that."

"Maybe," said the Village Mother. "But for the sake of your women and children it is better to live and be able to protect them in days to come than to save what you call your honor."

He said: "But if we stay here we will all starve together. In a few days the cattle will start to die. We must do something."

The Village Mother shook her head.

"If we are less strong than the savages, it is all the more important that we should show ourselves wiser. They must have food also. As our cattle run short of fodder, so they will lack meat. Then they must go away to find animals to kill."

"Some went away today, but others stayed behind. That is what they are likely to do next time, too."

"Then next time," the Village Mother said, "you may attack the ones that are left. There will be fewer of them, and they will not be expecting it. If you can drive them away, perhaps they will all go. They are not civilized people, as we are, who have a home that we love. They are mere wandering savages; and there are plenty of other places where they can find beasts to hunt. Perhaps they will go on once they realize they can get no advantage here."

Listening, Va hoped what she said was right. The others would go away, but Dom would stay in the wood. She would find him there and teach him all the things he needed to know, and after that bring him to the village. She rocked on her haunches and smiled secretly, thinking of it.

Three days later the opportunity which the Village Mother had spoken of came. Early in the morning scouts reported that many of the savages were moving away down the valley. The men wanted to open the gap in the hedge at once and go out to attack the ones left behind, but the Village Mother said no. They must wait until those who had gone were too far away to hear the cries of their friends, and run back.

An hour later the men begged again to be allowed to give battle, but the Village Mother still refused. When one protested, saying that the hunters must be more than five miles away by now and well out of earshot, she said:

"There is something else. I have noticed that they

drowse in the heat of the afternoon, like all hunting beasts. That will be the best time to surprise them."

Some of the men grumbled a little, but they would not go against the counsel of the Village Mother. So they waited, while the sun rose to its zenith and began its downward path toward the western hills. Then the Village Mother gave the word, the stone and the thorn branches were pulled to one side, and the men of the village ran shouting against the enemy.

It was soon over. Those left behind in the village heard cries of triumph from familiar voices, and went out to find them victorious and the savages all chased from the clearing. But they wasted no time in rejoicing. Following the instructions of the Village Mother they at once led the cattle out to graze, and collected fodder for the days ahead.

The Village Mother said: "If they have sense they will not come back, but go elsewhere to do their killing and leave us in peace. But if they do return they will still need to go away some time to hunt. When that happens, you can beat the ones they leave as you did today. We must be patient, and in the end they will depart."

They waited until evening to celebrate the victory. One of the cows was killed for the feast. The girls trailed chains of flowers over the beast, and the Village Mother asked pardon of the animal's spirit and then, while girls fondled it, one of the men struck it a blow behind the ear with a stone held in a twisted rope, and it sank to its knees, not knowing it was killed.

After that the carcass, now no more than dead flesh, was cut up and roasted over the fire; and they ate it with spiced bread and drank beer made from herbs, and afterward ate fruit that the children had picked during the afternoon. Then they sang together in the quiet dusk. These were not songs of battle and victory, but songs about the good things of their life in the valley: about love and marriage, children and crops and animals, about the shifting rhythm of the seasons—winter and seed-sowing spring, summer and harvest-autumn. Songs about life itself, and about death which, coming in the fullness of age, was a good thing also.

Va sang with them and thought of Dom. The savages would go, and he would be waiting for her in the wood. She would make up a song about that and perhaps in days to come—long years ahead maybe when she was old—all the people would sing it.

Next morning, when the savages were seen on the hillside above the village, everyone laughed at first. They looked so silly up there, scrabbling away the dirt at the base of the huge boulder. The villagers called to them, asking them if they were looking for roots to eat, or would they eat earth as they had eaten dust in the battle the previous day? Only the Village Mother said nothing and looked somber.

But gradually, as the hours passed and the savages went on with their digging, the rest of the people grew more quiet. They watched in silence as the hunters clustered round the stone and heaved against it, trying to make it move. They shouted with relief when they saw that the stone did not shift, but relief turned to dismay as the savages went back again to their digging.

Va found the Village Mother sitting apart from the others. She said:

"Mother, do something. Save us."

The old woman did not speak for a moment. Va was shocked to see that tears welled in her eyes and ran down her wrinkled cheeks. She said at last in a low voice:

"There is nothing I can do, child. They will break through the hedge. After that our only hope will lie in the courage of our menfolk. And I fear that courage may not be enough against brute strength."

The villagers watched the savages heave on the stone again, and saw it rock and heard their enemy's distant shouts of joy. The savages dug and rocked, dug and rocked; then the stone toppled forward and down but only went a little way. And some cried that they would be safe after all—that the stone was too irregular in shape to be rolled down the hill. They were still saying this when it began to move again, traveling faster and faster, lifting from the hillside and banging down as it hurtled toward them.

The men of the village rushed to that part of the hedge where the boulder would strike. For a moment or two it was lost to view behind the thorns, its presence marked only by the thunder of its passage and the cloud of dust thrown up behind it. But in the next instant the hedge exploded inward and the stone broke through, scattering men as though they were children's dolls.

Behind it came the shrieking, howling savages. The men of the village joined battle with them, but it was hopeless from the beginning. One by one they fell under the onslaught of the great white clubs of bone which crashed and crushed them down. Others did their best to fight also—old people, women, girls and boys—but they were brushed aside. They were so strong, these savages. Even without their clubs they would have triumphed, by the strength of their arms; with the clubs they were irresistible.

Va herself tried to oppose one shouting warrior, and was beaten to the ground by a flailing blow that drove the breath from her body. By the time she managed to get to her feet again it was almost over. In a couple of places a handful of men from the village still fought on, but for the most part the savages roamed unchallenged. Where they found a man still living they smashed his skull with their clubs. Va covered her eyes, but could not stop her ears against the groans of the dying.

She went to look for the Village Mother, and found her by the spring, lying with her legs trailing in the water. Va dragged her clear and cradled her head in her lap; her face was bloody from a blow which had crushed the side of her face. She spoke mumbling words at first; then said:

"It was my fault."

Va rocked her gently. "No, Mother."

"My fault," she said again. "I am Village Mother and I failed you. I failed you all."

"There was nothing you could do," Va said. "You could not stop them uprooting the stone, nor stop the stone breaking through the hedge. It was not your fault."

"I thought they would go away, but it was because my hopes deceived me. I knew what I should have done. They were stronger than our men, who could not hope to stand against them. We should have fled secretly while we had the chance. I thought of it, but if we had fled we should have had to leave our huts and our cattle and hens. Most of all, we should have had to leave this place which has been our home. So I kept the people here, hoping the savages would get tired of trying, and go on."

She coughed. Blood bubbled from her mouth and Va wiped it away. The Village Mother whispered:

"Hoping is not enough, and people are more important than cattle and huts. One can find more cattle, build more huts. One can make a new home."

She struggled to speak but the words would not come. Va knew she was dying. She said:

"Rest, Mother."

The one eye that could see looked at her.

"Get away, child, while you can." Her voice was very faint. "Go through the hole the stone made in the hedge. Escape into the valley. It may be that one or two others of our people will escape also. If so it lies with you, who would have been Village Mother in due time, to guide them to some place the savages have not found. Promise this, and I will rest."

Va said: "I promise."

"Then go!" With an effort she raised her voice. "Go now."

It was an order that had to be obeyed. Va eased her head down gently and slipped away, making for the place where the stone had crashed through. But when she got near she saw that it was too late—a couple of the savages stood on guard there, leaning on their blood-smeared clubs. There was no way out.

She thought of returning to the spring, but did not. The Village Mother was dying: there would be more peace in her death if she believed Va had escaped. Instead she went in search of her mother and found her in a group of women and children; but not before she had also found the bodies of her father and her brother. Her brother had been two years older than Va, a boy who laughed a lot but whose face now was twisted in the grimace of death that had come as the club smashed his skull.

Va went to her mother's arms. She did not say anything, either about the bodies or the Village Mother. There was too much to say, and nothing any good. They held each other, quietly crying.

She heard a harsh voice nearby, the voice of one of the savages. Frightened, she turned to look.

All she saw first was the club. Sunlight flashed from it except where blood had dulled the brilliance of the surface. She wondered if the savage would kill her, too, and felt she did not mind. Death might as well come now as later.

But he spoke again and this time there was something different, something in the voice that she knew. She remembered the same voice crying after her as she ran away through the wood. It was Dom. She would not believe it and looked at the face for evidence that it was another. It could not be Dom that stood there, holding that bloody club.

Yet it was he. Staring, she recognized him more plainly; dropping her eyes she saw the scar, almost healed, of the wound she had cared for. She looked once more at the club, stained with the blood of her people, perhaps of her father and brother, and then with loathing into his face.

He raised the club and, thinking he was about to strike her with it, she cowered away. Instead he put it in his left hand and grasped her arm with his right. He was trying to make her go with him—Va held back, but he dragged her forward.

Another savage, bigger and fiercer than Dom, came up. Dom spoke to him with his hand still on Va's arm, and the big man replied. When Dom spoke again, the other laughed, and the sound, ugly and cruel, made her shiver.

She could see something like fear in Dom's face as well, but he answered back. Then, after they had exchanged more words, he pulled hard on Va's arm, trying to drag her away. The big man roared in fury and struck at Dom with his fist, and Dom let go her arm to dodge the blow. It did not save him: a second powerful blow smashed against his head and he dropped without a cry.

The big savage took her arm as Dom had done, but far more brutally; his was a strength she had no hope at all of resisting. He dragged her to the door of a nearby hut and threw her in, sending her spinning to the floor. Va lay there helpless, too stunned and wretched even for tears.

Other women and girls were thrown into the hut. One, a friend of Va's, told her they were killing the cattle, all of them, cruelly and wastefully. She had also seen them killing the older women, and any younger women and girls who got in their way. The more they killed, the more furious and savage they became. At least those in the hut were out of the way of the slaughter; whatever might happen afterward, it was the safest place at the moment.

Va listened to her dully. She supposed that what she said was true, but it did not seem to matter. The rest of their people had been murdered, along with the innocent cattle, and obviously they would be murdered eventually. Death might as well come now as later.

But she stayed in the hut because despair and misery robbed her of any urge to move. She lay huddled on a bridal mat, woven in brightly colored strands of cloth, and remembered the wedding for which it had been made and how she and the other girls had helped in the weaving. The woman to whom it had been given was not in the hut; most likely she lay dead somewhere outside. There would be no more mats, no more celebration of weddings, no more of anything. All was ended.

A figure appeared in the doorway: a savage, she saw, and though she had thought she was resigned to being killed felt her stomach contract with new terror. Then she realized it was Dom again, and turned her head to the wall. He called her name, and she did not answer. She heard him moving cautiously about the hut. A hand reached down and moved her head, though not roughly. In the dimness of the hut, Dom's face looked into hers.

He spoke. His tone was urgent—wanting something—but the words in his savage tongue had no meaning. Va stared and did not answer. When he spoke again she shook her head and once more tried to turn away.

Then, haltingly, he used the words she had taught him when they played the naming game in the wood.

"Va . . . Dom . . . water . . . flowers . . . fruit. . . ." His face was twisted, trying to convey meaning. "Dom—Va . . . run!"

She guessed what he wanted. He would help her to get away from the big man; they would escape together. A day ago it might have been what she would have wanted, too—perhaps more than anything else. But that was before the stone crashed through the hedge and the savages came after it, shrieking and killing, killing. . . . Dom still held his club, and even in the shadowy light of the hut she could see the marks on it.

He pulled at her hand, and Va shook her head. The village was destroyed, all her people dead or about to die. She might as well die with them.

Dom tugged at her, but less roughly than he had done out in the open, and he kept his voice low. Probably he did not want to attract the attention of the big man and be knocked down again—she saw there was a swelling under his eyes. She said, allowing the loathing to come into her voice:

"I will not go with you. I hate you, who have helped slaughter my people. If you try to make me go I will scream, and the big man will come and strike you. Perhaps this time he will be angry enough to kill you. I would be glad of that."

Although he did not understand her words, she knew he could tell what her feelings were. He spoke in his own tongue, his voice urgent.

"Go away," Va said. "You and your kind have destroyed everything. You are a savage, like the others. The Village Mother was right when she said I should have left you to die. Now she is dead herself."

Tears stung her eyes. She remembered the Village Mother lying in her arms by the spring, and how she had blamed herself for not telling the people to flee while there was time. Her voice echoed in Va's head:

"Get away, child . . . escape into the valley. . . ."

Others might have managed to escape before the savages set a guard over the gap in the hedge. Once clear she might be able to run away from Dom and find them. It had been the last command the Village Mother had given her: to guide them to some place the savages had not found. She had promised her she would do that.

Va looked at Dom. She said:

"All right—I will come with you."

He could tell the change in her tone. He tugged at her arm again, and this time Va got to her feet and followed him.

7

WHEN DOM RECOVERED HIS SENSES AND got unsteadily to his feet, there was no sign of either his father or Va. The killing was still going on, and he could see the hunters in among the cattle, felling them with their clubs. There would be far more meat than the tribe could eat, and most of it would rot. They went on with the clubbing because the cattle simply stood there to be killed, lowing but unable to escape, not really even trying to get away. And also because of the lust which was in the hunters' blood by now, driving them on to further slaughter.

Dom might have felt it in his own blood if he had not been so shaken by what had happened. The blow had been staggering in itself. He had been cuffed often enough as a boy and sometimes knocked down, but this was the first time he had felt the full force of his father's strength. He understood the reason for it: he was no longer a boy but a hunter, and a hunter who offended the chief could not hope to escape with a slap as a boy would.

If he offended again his punishment would be more severe still. His father had wanted a son, but only a son who obeyed him. Any rebellion would provoke his anger even more than a rebellion by one of the other hunters. But to knuckle under meant losing Va; his father had taken her for himself and would never give her back. Dom rubbed his aching face. It was futile to think of fighting him. He was the strongest man in the tribe, Dom the youngest and weakest of the hunters.

On the other hand he could not contemplate giving Va up. If only they had stayed in the wood together. . . .

He looked and saw his father's huge figure among the cattle, flailing with his club. But where was Va? He heard the moaning of women from inside a nearby tree-cave, and peering in saw girls huddled together. He called "Va" and got no answer, but went in anyway and made them show their faces. One was Va. He spoke to her, telling her that they must go away together, back to the wood. She did not answer: even when he used the words she had taught him, she looked away. She did not speak until he tried to draw her out of the hut, and then her voice was filled with hatred.

He saw it was no good—she would not come with him freely and he could not take her by force. But as he was beginning to despair she spoke again, in a different tone. He did not know what had caused the change and did not care: the change itself was all that mattered. He pulled at her arm and she came, willingly if not eagerly.

Outside the hut Dom looked to see what was going on in the village. The old ones and the women and children of the tribe had come in also now, and were walking about. They gave small cries—of satisfaction at the sight of the sprawling bodies of the enemy, and of interest at all the things they found:

stone knives and hammers, pots, cloths and woven mats. Some were clustered round the fire, fascinated by the way it was held in and tamed by stones. A piece of wood fell and sparks flew upward, making them draw back in sudden terror.

The hunters were still occupied with the killing of the beasts, except for the two Dom's father had set to guard the gap in the hedge and make sure no one from the village escaped. Dom motioned Va to stay close in the shadow of the hut, and walked toward those two.

"My father sent me," he told them. "The enemy are all dead and there is no need for you to stay here. You are to go and kill the beasts with the others."

They went gladly, swinging their clubs and giving the hunting cry. Dom ran to where Va was and took her hand.

"Come quickly!"

Together they ran through the hole the stone had made. That was my doing, Dom thought: if I had not had the idea we would not have been able to get into the village and conquer it. Perhaps the other hunters would have killed my father, as the old women said they once before killed a chief. And yet he would not let me have this girl, and almost broke my jaw for disputing it.

But he knew that such thoughts were valueless. The tribe was victorious and the victory had set a new seal on his father's authority. His father was the chief and must not be disobeyed—he had said he wanted Va and that was enough. No one must defy him, least of all his son. If they were caught now he would almost certainly be killed.

His father might already have noticed, despite the frenzy of killing, that the guards had come away from the place where he had put them; in which case they would have told of the lie by which they had been tricked. He and Va were out in the clearing and had no cover. He pointed to a small clump of bushes, a hundred yards away, and urged Va to run in that direction. She needed little urging and ran fast at his side.

He did not stop at the clump but keeping this as a screen between them and the village ran on toward denser undergrowth. Not long after they reached it he heard shouting in the distance, and guessed that the chase was on. He told Va: "Run faster," but she was already doing so.

Gradually the shouts grew fainter. Good hunters though they were, they could not scent their prey as a lion did, and in country like this few marks were left by fleeing feet. They would be fanning out, he guessed, beating through the undergrowth surrounding the clearing. Every moment put a greater distance between them and their pursuers.

They came to the outskirts of the wood as the sun's rim touched the western hill. It had been a long day, Dom thought—morning and the struggle to move the stone seemed an age ago. He realized when they at last stopped running that both his arm and his face were hurting, and the wound in the arm was looking red and angry. He showed it to Va, and said:

"Find the plants to make it better, as you did before."

She said nothing. He used the words she had taught him. Pointing to the wound, he said:

"Plant . . . arm."

She still did not speak, but he was sure she knew his meaning. He cuffed her, not too hard but enough to make her wince and shrink away. He said, more threateningly:

"Plant! Arm!"

He watched as she searched among the bushes and found it. She bandaged his arm as she had done before, and Dom realized something else—that he was hungry. He thought of the fresh meat on which the tribe might now be feasting, and saliva ran in his mouth. He would have to make do with what there was here. He said to Va:

"Fruit . . . eat."

She gathered fruit for him and he ate some while she stood with her head bowed. That was the way it should be, the way a woman should attend a man. He said to her:

"You eat, too."

She made no reply, so he put one of the fruits in front of her mouth and spoke her words:

"Va . . . fruit . . . eat."

She shook her head. She was not hungry, he supposed, and ate the rest of the fruit himself. Dusk by this time was growing in the wood; the shadows thickened and birds sang their evening songs. Dom was tired: the day had been arduous as well as long. Va still stood before him with her head hanging, and he thought of the moss-bed she had made for him.

He could not remember the name in her language, so he lay down and then got up again and pointed to the place where he had lain. She either did not understand or pretended not to, but when he had cuffed her she found mosses and leaves and made the bed.

He told her to make another for herself and she shook her head again; if she preferred to sleep on the hard ground, he thought, that was her concern. He himself lay down in the softness of the moss. She squatted nearby, not looking at him. The sound of the birds died away into the quieter noises of the night, and the last flush of daylight gave way, bit by bit, to the softer glow of the moon.

As he lay there Dom reflected on the day which was ending. It was not easy to think clearly because so much had happened, and it had all been so confusing. But one thing he knew, and the reminder of it was like a cold fist clenched about his heart: he could never go back to the tribe.

The thought itself was like death—no one could live away from the tribe, no one ever had. A person who was cast out or abandoned or lost must perish. That was as certain as anything could be. In panic he wondered if even now there might be a way of avoiding such a disaster. If he were to go back in the morning, and give Va to his father, and bow his head in obedience. . . . It was no good. The die had been cast when he took her away: they would kill him on sight.

Nor even now, for all his fear of loneliness and helplessness, could he contemplate giving her up. She was his: no one, not even his father the chief, must be allowed to take her from him.

And thinking this he wondered if it might not after all be possible to go on living without the support of the tribe. The ones who had died had died in the grasslands, where there was little water and food could be obtained only through the hunting of game, and then only by the combined cunning of all the hunters. This land was different: greener and richer, full of trees which provided sustenance as well as cover. Fruit was not as good as meat, but one could live on it for a time.

The thoughts comforted him a little. Although he had cut himself off from the tribe he was alive, and he had Va. They would find a way of living; all the things she knew would help.

Drifting into sleep his ears, tuned by hunting skill to catch the least whisper of a movement through grass, caught a sound that was neither the distant passage of an animal nor a cat's faraway yowling. It was nearer, much nearer. At once, alerted, he came back from sleep, but he did not move. He peered instead through low-lidded eyes as Va, all the time watching his unmoving figure, got stealthily to her feet and began to steal away.

When she was a few yards from him she turned her back, and Dom rose to his feet. She heard him and started to run, but he ran after her with all his strength. She was his—he had given up the tribe to get her and he was determined not to lose her now. He brought her down, gasping and struggling, crashing into a bush.

Then, in the moonlight, he beat her, as all his life he had seen hunters beat women who dared disobey a man's command. He did it more coldly than in anger: she must learn, as all women must, that a man was her master, and that he, Dom, was that man. She did not struggle or cry out, only moaned softly as the blows landed. When he had finished she lay sobbing quietly, almost under her breath.

She might still try to run away, Dom thought, and he could not stay awake all night to watch her. So he took the belt she had around her waist, and tied one end round her neck and the other to his own belt. He went back to bed, dragging her roughly after him, and when he lay down she was forced to lie at his side. Tiredness soon overcame him after that, and he slept.

In the morning he made her find more fruit. When they were in the wood before they had done this together—now he must show her that he was the master, so he stood and watched her and took the fruit she gathered for him. He offered her some again, after his own hunger was satisfied, and as before she shook her head. He shrugged—when she was hungry enough she would eat.

She did whatever he told her, only nodding or shaking her head in response to his commands. When they went on he made her follow a few paces in the rear; far enough behind not to be able to attack him unexpectedly—though he did not think she would do anything so foolish—and near enough for him to catch her easily if she tried to get away. Occasionally he looked back and saw her walking there, with bowed head and closed unhappy face.

His arm was feeling better but he got her to replace the bandage. Watching her do this, with the hot sun bursting through the leafy cover and birds singing all round them, Dom felt a surge of confidence. She knew so many things which women in the tribe had not known. Even now, when she was being sullen and silent, she was useful to him, and when she realized that she could not run away and accepted him as her master, everything would be so much easier. Life would be as it had been the other time in the wood—all playing and smiles and laughter.

He led the way to the pool, and when they reached it pointed to the water and made swimming motions with his arms. She looked at him dumbly. He did the movements again, pointing at her and then at the pool. She shook her head.

The thought of the coolness of the water was

tempting, but he knew that if he went in himself and left her standing on the bank she might seize the chance to run away. He pointed once more to her and the pool and nodded his head vigorously, but she still shook hers. Then, with a flail of his arm, he pushed her so that she fell in. He thought of the time he had put his hand down to her and she had pulled him in. Afterward they had laughed about it, but there would be no laughing today.

As she stood up he jumped in beside her, glad of the liquid freshness flowing against his skin. He thought again: this is a good land. He did the clumsy swimming strokes she had taught him, moving out into deeper water. Va followed him as she had done on land, but here more smoothly and powerfully.

Dom was looking ahead as he swam doggedly toward the far bank, where the stream splashed into the pool over its ledge of rock. Then something caught his leg, dragging him down—a water-beast, he thought, as he floundered in panic and felt the water close over his head. He opened his mouth to cry out and choked instead. He kicked out his legs against that which was holding him just above the ankle but could not break the grip. He knew what it was, though: no water-beast, but Va. Her hand was grasping him—she was pulling him down to make him drown.

When he realized that, he stopped trying to rise to the surface, and instead plunged deeper and struck out with his fist at the place where she must be. The yielding element of the water confused him, but he felt his fist make impact with less yielding flesh. He was choking still and his ears were roaring but he punched a second time, savagely, and felt the hold on his leg break.

He came up, gasping and spluttering, vomiting water, and it was a moment or two before he was sufficiently recovered to look for Va. He saw her swimming strongly away from him, almost at the far side of the pool. Having failed to kill him, she was trying to escape again.

Desperately Dom lumbered after her through the water, threshing and splashing his way to the bank. By the time he got there and heaved himself out she was far away in the wood, a distant running figure among the trees. He shouted after her, but she did not check in her flight and he wasted no more time but went after her.

It was a long chase but by now his leg was well again and his strength greater than hers. He followed her through the wood and out onto the open slope below, the gap between them narrowing all the time. A brightly colored bird rose squawking from a bush as she crashed through it, and farther on two small pigs scattered away in the long grass.

She looked back and faltered, and he knew he had her. In another couple of minutes he caught her—she stood with shoulders bowed, awaiting chastisement.

The previous day he had beaten her coldly, as something that had to be done to teach a necessary lesson. This time he was bitterly angry. She had not only refused to learn the lesson, but had tried to kill him, her master. She fell to the ground, moaning, and he lifted her by her long hair and beat her again.

It was a distant sound that stopped him at last. It came from farther up the valley, from the direction of the village. He had heard it before, many times, and it had filled him with excitement, but today it chilled his blood. It was the cry of the hunters in the chase.

Va heard it, too, and looked up at him, shivering and sobbing. He said, speaking to himself:

"It may be they are hunting game. But usually they go farther afield—there is not much game left here in the valley."

She stared at him, uncomprehendingly. After a moment the cry came once more.

"And if it is not game they are hunting . . ."

He gestured abruptly to her to follow him, and she obeyed meekly. They went back up to higher ground, the small hill which was crowned by the wood. There was one spot which afforded a view a good way along the valley. Dom shaded his eyes against the sun, and peered southward.

He picked out a single dot first, then a second, eventually many. They were half a mile away, he judged, and heading this way.

They were spread out across the valley at intervals of about fifty yards. It was the formation and the maneuver used by beaters to drive game toward the waiting hunters; but if that had been the object the hunters would have been in position roughly where he and Va now were. So they were not beaters but hunters, and knowing that, Dom knew what quarry they sought.

If Dom had merely gone away from the tribe, his father would have let him go unhindered; but he had taken Va with him and Va was the property of the chief. So his father was leading the hunters in a chase that was not for game but for Dom and Va— to kill one and repossess the other.

They could not stay in the wood, which offered no protection against men whose eyes and ears were as keen as his own—no, keener. They could not stay in the valley, even, because the hunters would scour it from end to end.

He drew Va down into cover and crouched beside her. It was lucky they had not been spotted already. If they had been, those distant dots would not have been moving so slowly—the chase would have been on at full pelt, and Dom had no illusions about the way in which it must end. He might be able to outrun a girl, but there were a dozen at least among the hunters, including his father, who could even more easily run him down.

He said to Va, whispering although they were well out of earshot of the hunters:

"We must get away. And they must not see us. Follow me, and stay under cover."

She looked at him silently. Dom slipped away through the thicket, beckoning her to follow. For a moment she seemed to hesitate; then she came.

8

THE WOOD, WHEN THEY GOT THERE AFTER fleeing from the village, was an entirely different place for Va. In the past it had been special to her; her mother and the Village Mother had known that she went to it but not even they had ever gone there with her. The wood had been a place to be alone and private; to enjoy times of happiness, more rarely to console herself when her heart was sore.

And in the wood the most important part was the pool, where she had bathed, or fed the squirrels with nuts, or simply sat and thought. It had seemed

right that it had been at the pool that she had found
Dom, because the pool was an abode for dreams and
wonders.

After having it to herself for so long it had been
strange, but good also and exciting, to have someone
to share it with. She had loved it very deeply in the
past but those two days with Dom—the nursing and
the teaching and the playing—had been the best of
all. Even what had happened at the end—the killing
of the squirrel—although it marred the memory,
had not destroyed it.

It was destroyed now, though, and the wood
itself changed beyond recognition. It had turned
into a place of gloom and horror, almost as much so
as the desert of death that had been her home.
When, after he had eaten, Dom offered her some of
the fruit she had picked at his command, she could
not possibly have taken it. It was not just because of
her misery or her hatred of him: everything here was
poisoned, and she would have choked on the fruit
she had once loved.

She made his bed as he ordered her, and sat on
the ground near him. She thought of all those she

had loved whom Dom's tribe had murdered—her mother and grandmother, father, brother—and all those who had been her friends, like Gri.

Yet she had not seen Gri's body. It was true that she had not seen all the slain—in the end she had averted her eyes from the ugliness of the slaughter—but it might be, as the Village Mother had suggested, that some had escaped in the first confusion. Gri might have escaped. If she could only find him they could go away together to a different land, forgetting the piles of corpses and remembering only the living—helping each other to remember.

First, though, she had to be free of Dom. She watched him in the moonlight, waiting for signs that he was asleep, and at last heard his breathing become quiet and deepen. When she rose carefully to her feet, watching still, he did not move. So she began to creep away from the clearing and then, hearing him rouse up behind her, ran hard through the black and silver trees.

The beating he gave her when he caught her hurt, but it was not so bad as the feeling inside herself of having failed, and in doing so having failed the

Village Mother. Nor as bad as the humiliation of the belt being roped round her neck, and of being forced to lie yoked to someone whom in her mind she no longer thought of as Dom, but as this savage. He was asleep quite soon, properly so now, but she lay awake for a long time. If she had still had her stone knife she would have plunged it in his throat or breast, but she had nothing except her bare hands. And she knew her touch would waken him, and that against his strength she was powerless.

She slept at last, and woke and slept and woke, fitfully, through the long night.

The pool next day was like everything else here, as repulsive to her as once it had been inviting. But after he had pushed her in the water and jumped in after her, she had an uprush of hope. Here his strength was lessened, and her physical skill the greater. And perhaps there might be a spirit in the pool which would aid her. So she dived deeply and caught hold of his leg, and tried to drag him under.

She thought at first she was succeeding, as he struggled in vain to free himself—she had taken a deep breath before she dived and was sure she could

hold out longer under water. But then, instead of trying to get away, he came at her, punching viciously,
and even here his strength prevailed. So she broke
clear and swam for the bank, climbed out of the pool
and ran.

She had a good lead this time and she ran hard, but
she did so with no real expectation of getting away. She
had failed in this as in everything else: there was no
friendly spirit in the pool, no hope or help anywhere.
She ran out of the wood and down the hillside, but she
knew he would catch her. When he did, and beat her so
savagely, she thought he might be angry enough to kill
her, and almost welcomed it. It had been silly to imagine that Gri might have escaped—he was dead like the
Village Mother, like all her people. What use could
there be in going on living? When the beating stopped
suddenly she looked up at him, waiting for it to start
again, even wanting it.

Then she heard the distant cry and knew what it
was that had checked him. She saw the anger drain
from his face, giving way to fear. He spoke, and
though she had no idea what he said, she heard the
tremor in his voice.

She followed him obediently back up the hill, and took cover when he drew her down. When he beckoned to her to come away with him she understood the gesture, and knew how great was his fear of those small dots farther up the valley—so much greater than her own because she had had her fill of fear and gone beyond it. She hated the hunters who were searching for them, but she hated Dom more because he had destroyed more, and a more precious thing, than they had. All she needed to do was cry out: they would hear her and come running. It would not matter what happened afterward as long as she saw Dom brought down and slain first.

For a moment she thought she would do that, and framed the cry in her throat. He beckoned her again, almost pleadingly. Then, really not knowing why she did so, she stifled the cry and followed him.

They traveled fast all that day and the next, Dom occasionally pausing on high ground to scan the horizon for pursuers. After that first sighting they saw none, but he kept up a frantic pace—running and walking, running and walking, rarely resting, impatient when they had to stop to look for food.

At night he was careful to find good cover; and at night he tied her to him again so that she could not escape. This time, weary from the day's exertions, she slept heavily. In the morning Dom was awake early, dragging her to her feet: they ran southward through the dim cool dawn.

After two days with no sign of pursuit, Dom permitted their pace to slacken somewhat. They had come, also, into more level country, where it was possible to see for a long way. There were few trees here, and those there were bore no fruit. Instead Va searched for roots that could be eaten and they stayed their hunger on them, very grudgingly in Dom's case.

When they had traveled several days across the plain the landscape changed again. There were more trees, though still barren of fruit, sandy soil with thin wiry grass, and many rocks. The loose earth was very hot in the sunshine, and tiring to her feet.

In the early evening, Dom killed a rabbit. He stalked it carefully, gesturing to Va to stay back, and had almost reached it when it took fright and tried to whisk away. He quickly flung his club, striking the animal as it ran, and despite her hatred she had to admire the skill with which he did it. He picked up the rabbit with a shout of satisfaction and displayed it triumphantly.

What happened next, though, sickened her utterly. He used his teeth to bite through the skin of the rabbit's neck and quickly skinned it with his fingers. Then he tore a limb off the carcass and, putting it in his mouth, vigorously chewed it. Va watched, fascinated and appalled by the sight. She had known he was a savage, coming from a tribe of brutal killers, but she had not dreamed he would be an eater of raw flesh.

He finished that leg, tossing away the bone, and ripped off another leg to eat. Then, pausing, he tore away a third limb and threw it in Va's direction. She made no attempt to catch it, and it fell on the sandy ground.

Dom spoke one of the words he had learned from her when she fed him fruit and berries by the pool.

"Eat. . . ."

He pointed at the rabbit's leg. Va turned away in

disgust, but she could still hear the noise of his chewing.

Darkness was falling, and he indicated that they would stay where they were for the night. He set Va to gathering grass to make a bed for him. The grass was thin, shorter than the grasses of the valley, and it took her a long time to get enough of it together.

Suddenly she felt very hungry—she had eaten nothing apart from a few roots much earlier in the day. The rabbit's leg lay where it had fallen when Dom tossed it to her. Hungry though she was she could not contemplate eating it raw, but a thought came to her. There was a dead tree not far away, its branches withered and bleached by the sun. She went to it and broke some off, and collected them in a heap on the ground.

Dom watched but did not try to stop her as she did this; nor as she twirled one pointed stick in the hollow of another. But he started back when smoke appeared, and gave a grunt of amazement when the smoke turned to flame and ignited the dry grass she held close to it.

She made the fire, building up from twigs to

thicker branches, and cautiously Dom drew closer. He pointed at the fire and asked her something, but she did not know what he was saying. Then he tapped his chest and said "Dom," and pointing once more to the fire, asked again. She knew he wanted her to name it but stared at him in silence. Naming belonged to their first encounter, to the happy past which his cruelty had destroyed.

But he stood over her and hit her: so she named it: "Fire."

"Fire," Dom repeated.

He put his hand down and she flinched, but he only touched her shoulder in what was plainly a sign of approval. She guessed then that his tribe had never known fire, except as an accidental thing. Even the Village Mother, she thought with misery, had not realized what savages they were.

When the fire died down Va put the rabbit leg in the embers. Dom watched her, silent again, his nose twitching as the smell of roasting rose in the night air. When it was done she hooked it out with a stick and allowed it to cool; then she took the leg and started to chew it.

The taste was good but she had little chance to

enjoy it; Dom spoke to her peremptorily and
stretched out his hand. Silently Va gave him the leg.
He held it under his nose for a moment, sniffing,
before he opened his mouth and started to gnaw at
it. He grunted again, this time with pleasure.

He ate about half the meat off the leg and then,
after patting her shoulder with his free hand in further approval, held out what was left. He was offering to let her eat it, but even though hunger cramped
her stomach she would not touch it, soiled by his
teeth. When she shook her head he looked as though
he might be going to hit her, but instead returned to
the leg and finished it off himself.

That night, his hunger satisfied and feeling secure
at last from pursuit, he used her body for his pleasure.
It was painful for her but no more than that: she
could not hate him more than she did already.

They went on, day after day, their journey no longer
urgent but steadily progressing south.

One day he had her make him a knife. They
were in a rocky valley littered with flints, and he
picked up one of them and said the word "knife" in
her tongue. It was not the right kind of stone and

she shook her head. Dom cuffed her, though not hard, and she searched for a stone that would be suitable.

She found one at last of the right size and thickness, and another jagged piece with which she could chip it. Dom sat close by and watched her as she worked. It was not easy—making knives required a skill that was developed by long practice—and the result, after hours of labor, was poor. The old men of the village, who were best at such things, would have laughed scornfully at the sight of it.

Dom, though, took it from her with evident satisfaction, pressing the point experimentally against his skin and touching her shoulder in a way which showed she had pleased him. Va stared at him, her face expressionless. The stains of her people's blood—the blood of her father and brother—no longer marked his gleaming club of bone; but she had not forgotten them, nor the horrors of that day. She had made the knife at his command—she would have liked nothing better than to drive it into his heart.

She tried to kill him with it that very night. The

knife was held in a slot in his leather belt, and while he slept she got her fingers onto it and cautiously eased it free. But he awoke while she was in the act, and twisted away from her like a cat. Involuntarily exerting his full strength, he dragged her after him by the noose around her neck. She almost choked as the thin leather cut deep into her throat.

After that, as was only to be expected, she was beaten. He was angry and the beating was severe, but once more the sense of having failed was harder to bear.

She had also shown him that, despite her apparent acquiescence, she was still not to be trusted. Although he wore the knife in his belt by day, from that point Dom took precautions at night, putting it out of her reach where they lay. It was impossible for her to get hold of it without disturbing him.

So they went on together, always traveling south. The land changed as they went—sometimes arid and rocky, sometimes grassland, sometimes thickly wooded—but was nowhere as rich and green as the valley had been. Finding water was frequently a problem, and once they went a whole day and most of the next without it before Dom's keen eyes traced signs that led them to a water hole.

For the most part they lived on roots, but occasionally Dom found game. Usually this was in the form of such small animals as rabbits, but once he killed a young pig. He used the knife to cut it up and Va turned her head away, expecting him to eat the raw flesh as he had done before. But he said the word to her—"fire"—and Va found dry sticks and made a fire among the rocks. Dom watched her as he had watched her make the knife, and when the fire was crackling took a stick himself and twirled it against another piece, trying to make the fire come.

He could not do it: this also was something which required a special skill and long practice. But fire no longer alarmed him, and he threw on more sticks to increase the blaze. Va remembered she had once thought how good it would be to teach Dom things . . . how long ago that was!

The scent of roasting pig rose pungently in the air. Dom was ravenously hungry, and began to gnaw a piece before it was really cool enough to handle, pulling it away as it burned his mouth, but as compulsively bending forward to chew it again. When the first edge had been taken off his appetite, he indicated to Va that she could have one of the other pieces which he had dragged out of the embers. She accepted this time, her own hunger unbearably sharpened by the smell. It was the first meat she had eaten since she left the village.

Later she wept. It was not from any particular recollection of grief, but from a sadness that suddenly and unaccountably overwhelmed her. Dom stared at her, puzzled, then came to where she sat. He spoke in his own language, his voice friendly rather than harsh. When she went on weeping he put his hand on her shoulder. She jerked away and threw it off, and expected him to hit her; but he only looked at her and shook his head in bewilderment.

Next day they saw people. Dom saw them first—his hunter's eyes were sharper than hers—and said something in a whisper that was a warning, fastening a hand on her wrist. He pointed, and she looked in that direction. It was open country, mostly rolling grassland studded with thorn bushes and now and then a small tree. Figures moved against the distant horizon: she counted more than ten of them.

She could see they were men, but that was all.

They carried things in their hands but at this distance it was impossible to make out what they were. Not clubs of bone like Dom's, at least. They might be stone knives, or something quite different.

So they were not Dom's tribe, who anyway could not possibly have come so far south yet. They might be people like her own: people with skills, who lived in huts and grew corn and vegetables and kept livestock; people who made tools, and pots out of clay; people who laughed and sang. If she were to cry out they might come and rescue her from Dom, and then she could live with them.

But she could not be sure of that. It might be that even though not Dom's tribe they were equally savage and cruel. She might only be exchanging this brute she knew for many she did not. She followed Dom's lead, therefore, and kept silent. They watched the men pass across their field of vision and go away to the west. Not until some time afterward did Dom indicate that it was all right for them to go on. Va, as always, followed him, a few paces behind.

One morning when he unloosed her she noticed that her belt was frayed at the point where it had been looped about her neck. She thought about this during the day, examining the frayed place surreptitiously when Dom's eyes were not on her. That night she stayed awake after Dom slept, and twisted her head until she could get that bit of the belt between her teeth. She chewed at it, careful to make no sound or movement which might wake him.

Although frayed the leather was very tough. Her jaw soon ached but she forced herself to keep on, resting awhile and chewing again. Her mouth was filled with the sour leather taste, which sickened her stomach. She heard night sounds all round: a jackal howled, briefly waking Dom, and she had to stop until he was once more soundly asleep. She knew that having started she must go through with it. Otherwise he would notice the marks of her teeth on the belt, and not only beat her but tie her more securely in the future.

She could scarcely believe it when the belt parted at last; and she lay there with the leather's sourness against her tongue and her heart pounding. She listened and heard Dom's breathing, steady and deep. Very carefully, moving barely an inch at a time, she shifted herself away from him. Once he groaned, and she froze into immobility, expecting a shout and a blow. Nothing happened. Gradually it became possible to move less cautiously, and so faster. She crawled through long grass and at last, trembling, stood erect.

She could just make out Dom's sleeping form— she watched apprehensively but he did not stir. The night was very dark, but there was a silvery glow in the east which showed where the moon would rise. Va walked in that direction, treading lightly and warily long after she was sure that the sound of her footsteps could not reach him. When the moon came up she had been walking for more than half an hour.

At last she was free of him. The moonlight fell on a vast sea of grass whose crest waved softly in a breeze: nothing moved anywhere. He could not find her now, could not possibly track her in country such as this. She had only to walk on, and by morning she would be completely and finally beyond his reach.

To the east, continuing the path which she had already taken? There the plain stretched away with no sign of anything to break the emptiness. West was no good because it would bring her back close to Dom, and south was the direction in which he had been taking her and in which, once he had given up looking for her, he himself would most probably go. North—the way they had come? But what was there for her there, except a trail of remembered misery that led, in the end, to her ruined home and the savages who had destroyed it?

East then—but what was there for her there, either? What was there for her anywhere? And she would be alone, having to find her own game if she wanted meat, and hunt and kill it. She had none of Dom's strength and skill in things like that; nor his keen eyes to spy out animals, or men for that matter, before she herself was seen.

Va stood unmoving in the moonlight. She was free of Dom, but what good was the freedom? She hated him as much as ever but at this moment, staring into the limitless dark, she knew she also needed him. Perhaps it would have been better to die with her people, but she had not died. She was alive and wanted now to go on living. It would be so much harder to do that on her own than with Dom's help; perhaps impossible.

She turned back, retracing her path. It was not easy with so few landmarks, but she saw a solitary bush she recalled, a jutting tooth of rock, a dead tree. It took her an hour to get to the place where he lay.

He was sleeping still. She went forward cautiously and stood over him. In the moonlight she saw the club and beyond it the knife, out of reach when she had been tied to him but no longer so. She could pick it up and stab him before he woke, avenging in his blood the blood of her father and brother. It was what she had most wanted to do, and nothing now stood in her way. She could kill him with a single thrust. And be alone.

She looked down at him and felt tears in her eyes, tears not of grief but of anger at her helplessness. Still careful not to wake him, she lay down at his side as she had done before.

When she awoke it was light and Dom was bending over her. He pointed to the severed belt and she bowed her head, prepared for the beating which must follow.

It did not come though, and after a moment she looked up. He was staring at her, his face not fierce but smiling, and he touched her shoulder in the way which showed his approval. He knew she had tried to run away but changed her mind. He smiled and Va dropped her head again, hating him more than ever.

9

OM HAD NOT BEEN ABLE TO UNDERSTAND what it was that ailed Va. He presumed it had to do with the tribe's attack on the village, but that after all was something over and done with. She herself had come to no hurt through it: in fact he had rescued her from his father and the other hunters. It was true that he had beaten her—for running away and then for trying to drown him in the pool—but a beating was no more than any woman must expect, and for much lesser crimes than those.

There was no reason for her to keep up her sullenness, refusing the half of the rabbit's leg which he had offered her after she had shown how to burn it in the fire and make it taste good, having to be cuffed into naming things, sitting silent or weeping at the end of each day's trek. But reason or no, he learned to keep a close eye on her. After he had her make him the knife, he was prepared for her attempt to get it out of his belt and attack him with it. He surprised her groping hand, and then beat her again. He knew, though, by the look in her eye, that she had still not learned her lesson, and on other nights was careful to put the knife beyond her reach.

But the morning came when he awoke and felt a difference that for a moment or two he could not comprehend. It was not the presence but the absence of something—of the feeling of restriction to which he had grown accustomed since he had been tying Va each night to his belt. He missed the tug of another body as he turned over in the bed of grass.

He twisted round quickly, to see first, reassuringly, Va's sleeping figure; a moment later the severed strip of leather. Examining it, he saw the marks of teeth and realized what she had done. But she had not run away—she lay peacefully asleep beside him—nor attacked him while he lay defenseless. His club was where he had had left it, and the stone knife, too.

So at last she knew her place: that she was to be his mate and serve him as a woman should. It had taken her a long time to come to it, but now everything would be all right. Since she had not run away nor attacked him this time, he could be certain she would not do so. She might yet disobey or do foolish things and need to be beaten, but that was not important. What mattered was that she was his woman, and knew it.

He ought, he supposed, to beat her for chewing through the strap: clearly she had meant to run away, even though in the end she had thought better of it. A woman must obey, a man enforce obedience—that was the law of the tribe, handed down through the generations. But after pondering he decided against doing that. She had learned her lesson, and he could overlook this final defiance. He remembered the two days they had spent together in the wood and told himself that soon things would be like that time again. All they needed was to find a rich land, like the valley.

So Dom smiled instead of beating her, and patted her shoulder to show she was forgiven. He could not understand why she turned her face from him, but he was sure that everything was going to be all right.

But as they went on south they found no country as rich as that of the valley, and Va's attitude did not change. It was true he no longer tied her to him at night. And he had her make a second knife: it was better than the first so Dom took it, but he gave Va the first to keep, no longer fearing she might use it against him. They walked together, Va obediently a few paces behind, and ate together, and at night slept together. Yet she never smiled.

Gradually they came to understand each other's speech. The language they used was a mixture of those of both their peoples, but mostly that of Va's because she would only speak briefly, in answer to questions: the questions came from Dom and so the words themselves came from Va.

Once, while they rested after feeding well on a small deerlike animal he had run down and killed, he tried to get her to sing for him. He did not remember what the word for singing was, and tried to mimic the act as he had done that time in the wood. Then she had laughed at him, and afterward sung; now she only stared in sullen silence. When he beat her for that she wept but did not sing, and Dom's own heart was not in the beating. He had a strange thought—that there were some things, perhaps, which a person could not be made to do. Singing was one, and smiling another. When he was with the tribe, of course, there had been no songs and very few smiles. He did not think much about the tribe these days, and it was not easy to recall what that life had been like.

It came to him, as another new thought, that if beating did no good then kindness might. He did not really know what he meant by kindness: there had been no word for such a thing in his old language, and if there was one in Va's she had not told it to him. But it was to do with helping, as Va had helped him when she found him lying sick. If he helped Va, she might smile at him.

So instead of taking the first and best of the

meat from the next kill he made, as a hunter should, he gave it to Va. She looked at him uncomprehendingly, but he persisted and made her eat it. She did as she was told and took the meat, but did not smile. Another time he found flowers, white with golden hearts, growing in clumps near the place where they halted for the night. Va watched as he threaded them together into a necklace, but when he offered it to her she did not put it over her head but let it drop in the dust.

Dom was very angry when she did that. She deserved a beating, he thought, for refusing something which he had made and given to her. He raised his hand and she stared at him, flinching slightly but defiant. Maybe you could not force someone to take a gift, either, he thought, and his hand fell harmlessly to his side.

Their traveling took them onto higher land. There were huge pointed hills whose tops were white with a brightness they had never seen before, dazzling the eyes when the sun reflected from it. The days grew short and cold, the nights long and colder still. They shivered and clung together for warmth under their meager covering of skins, but though Va slept close to him at night, during the day nothing changed. There was sullenness always—no smiling, no words from her beyond what must be used.

One day she was attacked by a leopard. They had been drinking at a water hole overhung by trees, and Dom had failed to notice the leopard that lay crouched along a branch. It leaped at Va with a single coughing roar. She saw it in midair and tried to jump away, but its claws raked her shoulder and side. Dom had moved the instant she did, but forward not back, swinging his club with a roar of anger of his own. It was a lucky blow because he was unready and unsighted: he caught the leopard on the back of the neck and smashed it to the earth. Then he leaped on it, squalling and struggling still, and found its throat with his knife.

They stayed several days in that place while Va's wounds were healing. Dom himself did all the things that were necessary—skinning and jointing the leopard and roasting its flesh over a fire he made, and finding healing herbs to put on her wounds as she had once done for him. In the end, after the leopard's skin had dried in the sun, he gave it to her to wear, though it was the finest skin he had ever seen. She said nothing, and her expression did not change.

The cold grew sharper: it was as though the air had teeth. All one night they shivered, unable to sleep; and in the morning a whiteness drifted down out of the sky, soft like birds' feathers but melting damply on the skin. This, Dom guessed, was the same whiteness which lay on the tops of the high hills. It came down thicker and thicker, covering the ground so that their feet made holes in it as they walked. There was no sun—only a gray sky from which whiteness drifted, drifted.

Dom knew they must find refuge from it, and from the bitter cold. It would have been good to have one of the tree-caves there had been in the village, but failing that he must look for an ordinary cave. So he searched among the foothills and found one at last. It was a poor thing compared with the Cave where the tribe had lived in the rainy seasons: a place that one must stoop to enter and that was little more than a dozen feet in depth, but it offered shelter from the biting edge of the wind. They huddled together there and watched the snow, whirling now as the wind got up, blanket the valley below them.

It went on snowing most of the day. When it stopped late in the afternoon, Va went out and in the dwindling light hunted for dead wood beneath the snow. Although this was woman's work Dom went after her, and they brought sticks and branches back to the cave, and Va made a fire, coaxing the damp wood into smoke and, with painful slowness, into flame. They had no food but they sat close up against the fire and tried to warm themselves; then retreated to the back of the cave and lay together for comfort.

Next morning the air was a little less cold and the snow had disappeared, but Dom feared the possibility of its return. He felt he had been lucky in finding the cave and might not easily find another; so he told Va that they would stay where they were until the cold season was over. He went out hunting that day and came back, exultant, with a couple of rabbits. The fire had died down, but Va brought it to life again from the embers; while he was absent she had also gathered more wood and stacked it inside the cave. That was sensible of her, he thought, because the wood could be found more easily when it was not hidden by snow, and also because it would stay dry in the cave. He patted her shoulder, but she did not look at him.

They were there many weeks. The snow returned and stayed longer, and the cold deepened. One morning they went out to the stream from which they drank, and found it rimmed with thin plates of rock that one could see through. Dom broke some off and looked at the sun through it. It was so cold that it stung his fingers: he dropped it and saw it splinter.

The jagged edges were as sharp as the stone knife, sharper, and he wondered if perhaps Va could fashion a knife out of them; but they were so brittle that they cracked under the smallest weight. All the same he took several pieces back to the cave with him and left them near the fire. He was astonished later to see them turning into water.

Hunting was difficult and they very often went hungry, living chiefly on roots which Va found and grubbed up. It was a hard time, harder than any they had known since they had been together. They saw little of the sun. Even in the cave it was always cold, despite the fire which Va managed to keep burning. Then Dom fell ill.

He awoke one morning shivering. When he tried to move his legs were stiff and did not want to do the things his mind told them. He got up and went out of the cave into the snow, but fell down. Va came and looked at him.

"I am heavy," he said. "My legs are heavy."

She stared down at him. "You must come back into the cave."

"No." He shook his head weakly. "I must hunt. We need meat."

"You are ill," she said. "You lack the strength for hunting. You must rest until your strength comes back."

He had to have the help of her hand to get to his feet, and of her arm to get back into the cave. Va lay beside him and covered them both with skins and warmed him with her body, but he still shivered. Later she went out and found roots and made him eat them, but the sickness did not go. His head was burning hot, and she brought snow cupped in her hands and rubbed it gently against his forehead to cool him.

Dom had strange and monstrous dreams, worse than those he had when he was ill with the wound in his leg. In one, which came back over and over again, it was the day of the killing in the village; but he was fighting against the tribe, not with them. He saw the huge figure of his father, swinging the great club, and started to bow his head in automatic obedience before he realized that Va was there, too, and the club was raised to strike her down. Then, crying out in the dream, he rushed with his own club against his father, but knew he could not hope to beat him—no one could overcome such a mighty hunter. He cried out again, this time in despair, and felt his father's club smash against his skull.

His head throbbed as though from a real blow, and he called out hoarsely for Va. She knelt beside him, and cooled him as she had done before. He said:

"I could not save you from him."

"Rest," she said. "You are ill."

He took her hand and held it, small and cold in his hot grasp.

"Do not leave me, Va," he said. "Even though I could not save you, do not leave me."

But next morning when he awoke she was gone. He called her name a score of times, and no answer came. Hours seemed to go by while he drifted between fevered sleep and a wakefulness in which he knew his strength was ebbing. After a time he ceased to call for her. She had left him, he thought, because she too knew he was dying. He would no longer be able to find meat for her or protect her from wild beasts like the leopard; so she had gone away, as a woman must, to look for another man who could do those things.

With this in mind Dom prepared himself for death, hoping it would come soon. The fire died down from blaze to guttering glow and light ebbed from the sky beyond the cave mouth. He heard a noise outside and wondered if it was a hyena seeking prey: a dying man would serve it very well. Not until the figure loomed above him in the dimness did he recognize it as Va.

He cried out in astonishment and gladness. With more amazement still he saw that somehow she had contrived to kill a rabbit which she had brought back with her. She built the fire up with sticks and skinned the rabbit and jointed it. When it was cooked she gave it to him, sitting by him and holding his head and feeding him with the tender meat.

She gave him half the rabbit then and the remainder the following morning, taking none of it for herself. During the next few days his strength began to come back. Within a week he was well enough to go hunting himself and kill a small pig, which he surprised with others, grubbing for food beneath the snow.

In the feast that followed Dom insisted that Va take the choicest morsels. Later as they sat by the fire with full bellies, he said:

"You saved me, Va. Without your help I would have died."

She sat hunched and silent. Dom said:

"Sing for me, Va."

She looked at him and looked away; he saw loathing in her glance.

The snows melted at last, and two weeks went by without a further fall. The days were getting longer, the nights less cold. Dom said, one morning:

"The cave has protected us from the bad season, but now the bad season is over. This is a poor land, with not much game. It is time for us to go on, to find a place like your valley."

Va did not answer; it was almost as though she had not heard what he said. But when he went on she followed as usual, a few paces in the rear.

So they traveled south again, finding game where they could and living on roots the rest of the time. Twice they saw other people, hunters by the look of them, and on each occasion Dom was careful to keep away, and to take cover until they had passed. He knew they could not be his own tribe, even though one lot of hunters carried clubs of bone. It made no difference who they were because to any tribe he was a stranger, to be killed on sight as he would have killed a stranger in the old days.

The law of the tribe said "kill the stranger"—but it said other things as well. It said "beat your women so that they submit to the man who is their master." It had not been so with Va—he had beaten her but in her heart she had still defied him. Was he her master, after all? He did not know, but he knew what he most wanted—not that she should fear him but that she should smile, and sing as she had sung in the wood. He no longer beat her but the smiles and songs had not come and, he thought unhappily, never would.

They came down out of the hills and Dom stared in wonder. He saw water—such an expanse of it as he could not have dreamed existed, water that stretched out for more than a mile in front of them. It lay in shadow under a cloudy sky but as they got nearer sunlight broke through, turning the chill gray-green to gold-dazzling blue. With every step forward it seemed to increase in extent. They descended the last slope and stood on the shore of the lake, and the immensity of it was awesome.

They stayed there many days, always within sight of the great water. The warm season was coming back; there were rains occasionally which soaked them but they dried off quickly in the sun. At last Dom felt his full strength returning after his sickness in the winter.

But though the place itself was attractive, the prospects of game were poor: he found no rabbits and few wild pig. There were roots in plenty and trees which later might bear fruit—now they were pink and white with blossom—but not much chance of getting meat. The game, he decided, must range farther south; and if they did not come to so vast a water hole as this it meant the whole land there must be well watered. It was time for them to go on again.

When he had come to this conclusion, he told Va. It was a sunny morning and they were eating roots, along with the young green shoots of a plant which grew in abundance near the lake. His stomach longed for the richness of meat.

Va did not answer him but that was not uncommon. He stood up, expecting her to do the same, but she remained squatting a few feet away. He said:

"We are going on, to look for game. Come, Va."

She spoke then. "I am staying here."

"No." Dom shook his head. "We must go on."

"I cannot." Her eyes stared blankly at him. "I am heavy."

He remembered how his own limbs had been heavy, in the cave. He said:

"If you have a sickness I will look after you, as you looked after me. It is the warm season now, and the sickness will soon be over. Then we will go on."

"No. I shall stay in this place."

Dom looked at her, puzzled. She rose from her squatting position and stood in front of him. She placed her hand on the curve of her belly.

"This heaviness is not a sickness, I am with child: that is why I will not go on."

He gazed, understanding the words but scarcely able to believe what they conveyed. With child. . . . He went to her and put his hand on top of hers, feeling her warmth. With great joy he said:

"I shall have a son."

Va said nothing. Dom repeated the words, almost shouting in his happiness.

"I shall have a son!"

Va stared at him a moment, and turned away.

Now he had two things to care for—Va, and the child within her body. He cossetted her more than ever, seeking out good things for her to eat, finding moss and leaves and making a soft bed for her to lie on.

One day she said: "I shall need shelter for my baby."

Dom shook his head. "There is no cave near. I have searched for one."

Not a cave, she told him, but a hut. He did not know the word and she explained: one of the tree-caves such as there had been in the village. Dom said:

"I cannot make one."

"I will show you," Va said.

So she showed him which saplings to uproot, and how to strip them of bark and cut them to a proper length; how to fix them firmly in the earth and tie them with ropes of grass; how to make a roof using other saplings and cover it over with dried grass mixed with mud, and then fix big glossy leaves on top and all round the sides. It took him a long time—twice he had to start again from the beginning—but in the end the hut was built.

It had been built at a spot which Va picked, on the outskirts of a grove of trees and not far from the point where a wide fast-running stream emptied itself into the lake. It was a good place, Dom thought: she had chosen well. He looked at his work with pride.

That night they slept in the hut, and though before they slept they heard the rain beating down on the leafy roof they stayed dry and warm. It was good to listen in such comfort to the rain, good to know that Va was there beside him, good to know that her body sheltered his son. The gladness Dom felt was more like that first time in the wood than anything since had been; it had a feeling of safety in it.

He wanted to tell Va about this, to tell her how wise and good she was, to tell her that whatever happened he would protect her with his life: her and his son. And also he wanted to tell her of the delight he got from looking at her, how beautiful she was. But he did not know the right words. They had not existed in his old language, and though they might have done in hers she had not told him them. All he could do was speak of other things which gave him something of that feeling, things she had shown him.

"You are like the pool in the wood, Va," he said. "You are like the flowers I put around your neck."

It was a rainy dusk outside and even dimmer in the hut, but he was close enough to see the details of her face—broader than those of the women of his tribe, the cheekbones higher and the brown eyes

IO

VA'S FEELINGS, WHEN SHE REALIZED THAT SHE was pregnant, were of fear and loathing.

In the village the moment of a woman knowing she was carrying a child had been a prized and honored one. She would tell the Village Mother first, then other women, last of all her husband. That night the village made a feast, much like the feast for a marriage, and they sang together: songs of joy in the new life and hope for the future.

Va stared about her. In front lay the flat emptiness of the lake; behind, strange hills and stranger mountains capped with snow. The valley had been a rich enclosed space, the village a stronghold within it. Here was no valley and no stronghold, no Village Mother to tell, no woman who would rejoice with her and help her make the garments she would wear while the child grew in her. This was an open friendless place, the only person near her this man she hated—this slaughterer of her people, murderer of her father and her brother.

And father of her own child. She hated the child, too, for that, for being sprung from such a one. She would have had it wither inside her if she could.

For three days she kept her secret; only when Dom said they must go on, to find game, did she tell him. In his tribe, she supposed, the women had been accustomed to trekking on with swollen bodies and bearing their babies under a bush somewhere; but she came of a civilized people. A child needed a home, and a home was in one place. This was not the one she would have chosen, but nowhere was except the valley which the savages had ravaged and from which this one savage had taken her. But it was better at least than some of the harsh desert lands through which they had passed, and there was no certainty of their finding anything better.

Their finding, she thought bitterly, because she knew she still had need of Dom—more so than ever with the months of heaviness and ungainliness that lay ahead. If he had insisted on going on she would have followed before he was out of sight. But she knew also that he had changed in his attitude toward her, no longer beating her but instead trying to win her favor. So she told him she would go no farther and when he looked at her, puzzled but not angry, told him why.

The joy he showed at the news sickened her. "I shall have a son!" he shouted, and she knew him yet again for a savage. In the village sons were welcomed, as were all children, but it was counted a double blessing to bear a daughter first. She thought fiercely: this will be a daughter. My daughter.

But at least Dom's satisfaction completed the change which she had already noticed in him. He did things for her readily and continually looked for ways to please her. She told him to build the hut, and showed him how, and once even scolded when he did something wrong. She had a quick rush of fear the moment she had done so, but he showed no anger.

It was good to have the hut, good to be able to stay in one place instead of continually moving on. She found suitable stones and put them together to make a hearth, and kept a fire burning there even when she was not using it to roast their meat. She did not really need it because the weather grew warmer every day, but it was a sign of being settled and a recollection of the home she had once known.

Dom, of course, often had to go away to hunt game, which remained scarce in this area. Va was entirely happy then, busying herself with necessary tasks or simply staring out at the lake. It was altogether different from the valley, but she discovered it had a beauty of its own, marked by the changing tints of sunlight and shadow. She grew fond of it.

Day by day she found new things to do. There were flints along the bank of the stream which she chipped into knives, and she also found a big flat stone with a hollow in the middle which she saw could be used for pounding wheat into flour. She remembered then that farther along the lake she had seen what from a distance might be wild grain, and went back there and found that this was so. It was standing high, but green and small-eared. In a month or two it would turn gold and the ears hang heavy; then she would gather the wheat and grind it into flour, and so make bread.

There was also flax growing not far away. Remembering how her people had done it, she stripped the plants into fibers which she dried in the sun. Afterward she made a cloth from them, and a dress from the cloth. It was rough material and she had no dyes, but it was better than the skins she had been obliged to wear.

She tried to make pots. There was plenty of good clay in the vicinity, and she took some and laboriously fashioned it into the shape of a pot and set it in the fire to bake. But when the fire died down it was cracked, and even if it had been whole she doubted if it would have held water. She needed to have an oven, such as they had had in the village, to increase the heat of the fire and hold the heat within it while the clay changed into stone.

She would make one, she determined, though not just yet. The year had ripened and she had ripened with it, becoming very big, and slow and clumsy in her movements. Even getting up and down was difficult.

Dom looked after her more carefully than ever. When her time was approaching he did not go away hunting, but brought her fruit from the trees and berries from the bushes to eat. There were fish in the stream and the lake, and he tried to catch them but could not. They slipped away as he waded into the water, and when he threw his club at them from the shore it did them no harm.

One day Va knew her time had come. She thought, for an instant only, of the way it would have been in the village with all the other women to help and comfort her, and then dismissed the thought. She sent Dom away, and crouched in the hut and bore her child, and did the things that were necessary as best she could.

The child cried when she slapped it to make it draw breath, and Dom came to the door of the hut. He looked down at her anxiously as she cradled the baby in her arms. Then he reached his large hands down for the baby, and she gave it to him to hold. He looked at it, and she saw his face broaden in a grin of triumph. He cried:

"In all things you are a good wife. You have given me a son!"

Even in this, Va thought bitterly, she had failed. She had been sure she would bear a daughter.

Dom handed the child back to her.

"Take my son, Va, and feed him."

Mutely she took the baby and held it to her breast.

But though it was a boy, Va found that she loved the baby more than she had ever loved anything or anyone in her life—more even than she had loved the Village Mother. She fed him and cared for him and caressed him, rocking him to sleep in her arms. She crooned to him songs of lullaby, which the women of the village had always sung to their babies.

She was doing this one day when Dom came into the hut, and she stopped when she saw him standing there. He asked her to go on singing, but she looked at him with stony eyes; in the end he went away, and she could croon again to her baby. She called him Bel: it was the name of her brother who had been slain by Dom's tribe. She had expected Dom would have a name of his own for the child, but he called him Bel as she did.

The harvest time was over—leaves fell from the

trees, twisting in the wind, and the days shortened and sharpened. The cold season came again; but now they had the hut for shelter, and Dom had stacked wood in piles to keep the fire going during the winter. They had a store of meat also: Va had showed Dom the way they preserved meat in the village, not by cutting it into thin strips and letting it wither in the sun, but by rubbing in salt and hanging it in the smoke of the fire.

Dom still went hunting when the weather was not too harsh, sometimes to parts so distant that he was forced to sleep a night away from the hut. Va loved those times, when she and Bel were alone together, and she could sing to him with no fear of Dom appearing and drying up her voice. It saddened her when Dom returned, but he brought fresh meat and eating this made her milk good and put strength and vigor into Bel's small limbs.

One day Dom took him from her after she had filled his belly. She watched jealously, hating to see him in Dom's arms but knowing there was nothing she could do about it. He was Dom's son as well as hers, and Dom brought the meat that, through her body, sustained him.

Dom put his finger into the baby's hand and it closed into a tiny fist to grasp him. He laughed.

"He is a strong one, our son! You feed him well, Va. He will be a big man when he grows up."

She did not reply. Gently Dom freed his finger, and ran his hand along Bel's arm.

"He has good limbs, a good right arm. He will wield a mighty club when the time comes."

"No!" Va shook her head violently. "My son will not have a killing club."

"He must, if he is to be a hunter."

"Then he will not be a hunter. He will tame cattle, as my forefathers did, and grow wheat and other crops. When he has to kill an animal for food, he will do it with kindness and ask pardon of the spirit of the beast. He will not murder for the love of murdering."

She had spoken sharply. Dom did not reply at once. Then he said:

"He must be a hunter. The time will come when I am too old and feeble to protect you; then our son must do it."

"I will not have him made into a savage! He will be like my brother, whose name I gave him—a boy of happiness and gentleness and love."

Dom stared at her. "Your brother is dead."

She spat at him. "I know it, and you killed him!"

"He is dead because although he was gentle and happy and loving his right arm was not strong enough. Those may be good things, but without strength they are nothing."

"You killed him," she said. "For that I hate you, and always will."

He gave her back the baby, and his face was dark and unhappy.

"You have taught me many things, Va," he said, "and I have been glad of the teaching. And you have brought many good things into my life: most of all this son, and your own self. But what I said was true. Nothing can grow unless a strong arm shields it."

He went out of the hut to where the wind was blowing snow along the lakeside.

The snows melted and the air grew milder: days lengthened and the sun shone more often. Above the hut the trees and bushes put out fresh green points, which slowly uncurled into new leaves.

Bel grew bigger and stronger all the time. He talked and laughed, in his own tongue which as yet was neither Va's nor Dom's; and he learned to crawl, slowly and awkwardly at first, then more and more nimbly. Va did not have to carry him with her everywhere, and could do things while he played.

She found plants which were good to eat, or bore fruits that were, and put them together in a patch of earth near the hut, digging them in carefully as she had seen the men do in the village, and taking water to them in a shell when there was not rain enough. She had saved some of the seeds of wild grain from the previous autumn and she planted this, too, in a spot where she could tend it and pick it easily when the new seeds were ripe. She hunted along the shore, and found strange small animals in low water that had skins as hard as rock, but with flesh inside that was good and sweet once they had been baked in the fire. In the nesting season she gathered the eggs of the big birds that fed on the fish in the lake.

Often she stood by the lakeside watching them. They flew low over the surface of the water, probing it with keen eyes, and then plunged down like sharp-pointed stones, to emerge with fishes wriggling in their beaks. Va wished she were a bird and able to do that. When she waded into the water the fish fled away as they had fled from Dom, and all her skill in swimming could not bring them within her grasp.

One day, though, before Dom went off to hunt for game, he spoke of how much harder the hunting was than in the old days, when the tribe had sent out boys and old men to encircle the beasts and chase them down the funnel of beaters toward the waiting hunters. Now he had to run animals down by himself, with no help. There were antelope less than a day's journey to the south, but they were too fleet-footed for him to have any hope of catching one.

Va thought of this after he had gone, as she watched the fish that swam in the stream near the hut. They were speckled brown and yellow, about a foot in length, and they would stay for a long time in one spot, motionless except for the small beat of fins that kept them in place against the current. But if she put a toe in the water, or even let her shadow come between them and the sun, they turned and darted downstream, almost too fast for the eye to follow.

If someone were waiting down there, as Dom said the hunters had stood waiting for the antelope . . . ? She shook her head. The fish were so much smaller and moved too fast through the slippery water for anyone to catch them. But if there were something in the water to stop and hold them? A cloth? But they would see it, and draw back.

It was not until hours later, as she was plaiting grass into cords to mend the roof of the hut which the wind had blown awry, that the idea came to her. If one knotted many cords together, with holes between them not quite big enough for a fish to swim through . . . with the stream freely flowing through the fish might not notice it and might rush into it and be held fast. Then one could lift the net up and easily take out the fishes on dry land.

As soon as she had mended the roof she set to work to make a net. She did not finish it that day and was particularly glad when Dom did not return at night: this was an idea she did not wish to share with him. Early next morning she started again, with Bel crowing at her feet. When she had finished the net she took it down to the stream.

She had already marked a good place where the stream narrowed and ran more deeply. She realized the net would need to be anchored on either side, and hammered two sticks into the ground to hold it. The net lay across the entire width of the stream and the water flowed through it, unimpeded. Va looked at it with satisfaction, then went upstream to the spot where the fish hovered, nose to current.

With her foot she shattered the surface of the water, sending up a spray of silver drops which flashed rainbow colors in the sunlight. The fish twisted and darted, and Va ran down beside the stream in pursuit. But anticipation turned to disappointment as she reached the net—not a single fish was caught in it—and to gloom as she understood why: although the net came up to the surface of the water, it floated and so did not quite reach the bottom. The fish had swum underneath it and escaped.

Va took the net from the water and looked at it despondently. Then she realized what she must do—anchor it to the bottom of the stream as well as to each bank, so that it could not float up and leave a gap.

She waited until the fishes had resumed their place upstream before putting the net back in. She tried securing it with sticks, but the bottom of the stream was either too stony or too soft so the sticks would not hold. She was dejected again until she thought of anchoring it with heavy stones. She found several big flat ones and laid them in the stream on the lower edge of the net. That made it quite firm: not even a small fish could escape beneath it.

Once more she alarmed the fishes, causing them to turn and flee. But this time when she went to the net she found three big ones struggling in the meshes—the rest had been small enough to wriggle through. Happily Va unhooked the net and dragged it out. One fish got clear while she was doing that but the other two flapped helplessly on the bank. Making a brief prayer to their spirits, Va quickly killed them with a stone.

She cooked them in the embers of the fire and picked the bones clean with her teeth. The white flesh tasted very good—sweeter than animal flesh, she thought. She looked at the stream, where more fish had already gathered at their favored spot. Even when she had caught those, there were all the fish in the lake. She thought of Dom, hunting throughout a long day, perhaps, for one rabbit. This was an easier and better way of getting meat.

The idea came to her, as sudden as the idea of the net, that she no longer needed Dom. She had the plants growing in the earth, and a means now of getting fish from the stream. She had the hut for shelter, and Bel for company; without Dom she and Bel could be happy together all the time. She could sing to him with no one else hearing, and teach him things and tell him stories, and he would never have a killing club of bone. How good it would be!

When Dom came back that day, bringing a porcupine he had killed, Va was more sullen than ever. She cooked the porcupine for him, but refused to have any herself. Dom asked her if she was sick: she shook her head but would not speak to him.

She told him nothing about catching the fish, and she had hidden the net in the wood before he returned. If he knew the way of catching fish, she thought, he might not be willing to go and hunt far away. He would be there all the time and she would never be alone with Bel.

And if he continued to hunt, going farther and farther away, perhaps one day he would not come back at all. Perhaps he would lose his way, though that was very unlikely. Or perhaps a lion would eat him. She did not want to think about that, for although she still hated him the urge for revenge had gone since her baby was born. All thoughts of killing and death were hateful to her—even Dom's. But it would be good if he did not come back. She hugged her baby to her breast. It would be so good!

But Dom did not lose his way, nor get eaten by a lion. Regularly he went out to hunt, and as regularly came back with meat for himself and Va. She was glad when he went, unhappy when she saw his figure returning along the shore of the lake. Dom did his best to placate and coax her, but to no effect: she tolerated his presence, as she had to, but she yielded nothing.

The year turned. Spring gave way to summer, to days of sweltering heat when at times the only relief was to bathe in the lake as she had once bathed in the pool in the wood. Bel grew fast and agile, and she took him with her into the water, and held him up while he splashed and laughed and gurgled. Then they lay together on the hot sand of the shore, basking in the sunshine. Except for the thought of Dom returning it was a blissful time.

The plants grew in rows as she had put them in the earth, and the wheat lifted high and began to turn yellow with the promise of harvest. In the nearby woods red fruit hung from the boughs, and she found nuts that would soon be ripe. There were squirrels in the trees, and she thought that when the nuts were ready she might tame one, as she had tamed that other that Dom killed.

On a gray morning she thought of that, and of the greater killing that had followed—not of one small animal but of all her people. Yet it was very far away, the horror of it still there but faded in her memory. What mattered was that she was safe here, she and Bel.

Mist rose from the lake and spread out over its shores and up into the surrounding woods. A lighter patch showed where the sun was, though there was no sign yet of its breaking through. The air was still, not cold but dank to the skin.

Va decided to go and look for crabs—there was a section of the lakeside about a mile away, jagged with rocks, where she usually found some. She did not take Bel with her—he was asleep on his bed of moss—but put up the barrier she had made, out of sticks tied together with grass-cord, to prevent him getting out of the hut and crawling into some danger.

She realized again as she walked along the shore how much she had come to love the lake. Even in this mist it was beautiful. A few birds were singing higher up among the trees, and nearer there was the gentle lapping of water against the rocks; otherwise there was no sound except the crunch of her feet in the sand. Dom had been away since the previous day and was unlikely to be back before evening. She would catch a crab and take it back to the fire and bake it. Then, after she had eaten, she would play with Bel and make him laugh.

She reached the spot where the rocks were thickly clustered and waded out into the water. She found a big crab after a little searching, and almost immediately afterward a smaller one. She would eat well. Pleased with herself she carried them to the shore, their claws clashing futilely in the air, and looked for a stone with which to kill them. It was while she was so occupied that she heard a shout from farther along the lakeside.

When she looked she saw the club first, and thought with disappointment and annoyance that it was Dom returning early. But the voice had not sounded like Dom's, and he would have called her name. At that moment she saw that there was not one man, but two: strangers and, as their clubs made plain, savages.

She dropped the crabs and without thinking ran back the way she had come. She heard a second shout, and a quick look over her shoulder showed them both running after her. She tried to run faster, her heart pounding with fear as well as with the effort. Now both of them were shouting and their voices were harsh and terrifying: it was a long time since she had heard Dom's voice sound like that.

When she was almost in sight of the hut a thought more urgent than fear stabbed her—she was leading them to where Bel was. She glanced back again and saw that they were gaining on her. At once she changed course, running away from the lake instead of alongside it. She might lose them among the trees; it was her only hope.

She heard their shouts and the sound of their blundering progress behind her, but once they were in the trees she could no longer see them. Or be seen. If she were to hide and let them go past. . . . She found a dense patch of brush and crouched inside it, shivering.

They went past, one of them no more than a few yards away, and she waited with beating heart as the sounds grew faint. She felt a half-relief from fear, but it did not last. After a time there was the sound of feet crashing through the undergrowth again, and rough voices calling to one another. They had guessed what she had done, and were coming back to search for her.

Va was torn between the instinct to flee and the hope that they might not find her. Her indecision, sharpened by fear, resulted in her doing something which combined the worst part of either course: she waited until the savages were quite close, then suddenly ran.

With a shriek of triumph they were after her, the leader only a few paces behind. She ran as she had never run before, not even when she was fleeing from Dom in the valley, but it was no use. Feet pounded closer and closer in pursuit; then a hand grasped her hair and she was dragged brutally to the ground.

She looked up, sobbing, and saw them standing over her, grinning, holding their cruel clubs. She had no hope now, and her heart was seized by a fear and despair more terrible than anything she had known or could have imagined. For she knew they would find the hut, conspicuous as it was on the lakeside, and when they had finished with her they would kill Bel.

It was then, not from hope but out of the depths of her being—a cry formed by all the things that had happened to her since that day by the pool in the wood—that she shrieked Dom's name.

"Dom! Save me. . . ."

One of the savages reached down, taking a fresh hold on her hair, and hauled her painfully to her feet. She cried Dom's name again, and he dropped his club and smashed his fist into her face.

At that moment there was another roar, not from either of these, and a figure charged from the bushes, club in hand. So there were three of them, she thought, her head dizzy from the blow—it made no difference. But as she thought it, the club crashed against the skull of the savage who was holding her and he fell, dragging her down with him. Incredulously she saw that it was Dom who had struck down her attacker.

Howling, the other savage struck at Dom. Dom tried to dodge but the blow caught his arm and his own club dropped from his nerveless fingers. The savage yelled, a screech of victory, and raised his club to strike again—he was as tall as Dom but more squat, with powerfully muscled arms. Va saw that in the instant in which she heaved herself up from the ground and threw herself at his legs. It was like throwing herself against the trunk of a tree: she could not budge him. She could not even maintain a hold—she was kicked sprawling away, her remaining breath beaten from her lungs.

But she had enabled Dom to parry the second blow, and given him time to recover his club. The two men faced each other, growling their hate. With a new thrill of fear Va saw how much bigger the savage was than Dom: he looked twice as broad. He raised his club with a shout that shocked her ears, and brought it crashing down. Dom dodged, but only just. Twice more the savage struck, and twice more Dom was agile enough to make the blow miss.

But the eventual end was certain—Dom could not possibly overcome an enemy as big and strong as this. She must help him. Gasping for breath, Va tried to rise, and failed.

The savage saw her movement from the corner of his eye and glanced that way. It was only for a moment before he turned back to Dom, but the second distraction like the first gave Dom the chance he needed. He struck hard—the savage put up his club to fend off the blow and the club was knocked aside. Before he could raise it again Dom got in a second blow which caught him on the side of the neck and sent him staggering. As he fell back Dom went after him and hit him a third time, on the forehead. He crashed to the ground and Dom fell on him, stabbing viciously with his knife.

They left the dead savages as prey for the vultures and went back together to the hut. Bel was awake, and laughed and gurgled when he saw them. Va saw how beautiful he was, and knew how much she loved him; and knew also that but for Dom it would have been the savages who came here now, to murder him.

While she held Bel close, Dom told her how it happened that he had been at hand. He had first seen the two savages early that morning, many miles from the lake. Because they were heading in that direction he had abandoned his hunt and followed them, trailing them but keeping out of sight. He did not want to have to fight them, and hoped they would not go near the hut, perhaps not even go to the lake. It would be better if they traveled on undisturbed.

When he saw them reach the lake and go along the shore, he knew that they were bound to discover the hut. So he stopped following them and instead took a shortcut through the wood, to get to the hut first and take Va and the baby away. He found Bel but there was no sign of Va, so he went down to the beach and looked along the lakeside in the direction from which the men would be coming. That was when he heard Va's cry for help, and ran through the trees to her aid.

She said: "You saved me, Dom."

It was the first time she had used his name since the days in the wood in her own valley. She remembered that he had also saved her when she was attacked by the leopard: yet this was entirely different. She had not really cared whether the leopard killed her or not, but today she had cared. Because it was not just her he had saved—he had saved Bel also.

Dom said with a worried face: "The men might have come another way to the lake, and then I would not have seen them, would not have known there was danger."

She looked at him, her arms tight round Bel, and said:

"Do not go away again, Dom. We want you with us."

Dom shook his head. "I do not want to go, but we must have meat."

"The fishes' meat is good and sweet."

"Maybe. But they are too slippery and move too quickly through the water for me to catch them."

"I can catch them."

She told him about the net. He listened in astonishment, and said:

"You are very clever, Va. I would not have thought of such a thing."

"If we make a bigger net and wade out into the lake together with it, one of us at each end, and then draw it back to shore, we might catch many fish. The lake is filled with them, as is shown by the diving birds."

Dom nodded. "We can do that. And I will not

need to go away to hunt. I can be with you and Bel always."

"Yes."

There was no doubt in her mind that she wanted him to stay with them. The hatred she had felt for him was lost in her new awareness of thankfulness and gratitude, and a feeling of kindling warmth. The image of her dead brother came to her, bringing with it a quick sense of horror and loathing, but she put it away. His tribe had destroyed her people, but he had saved her and saved their son. She looked at him again in the way she had looked beside the pool in the wood, and saw beauty in the dark powerful lines of his face, in the piercing eyes and springing beard, in all the strength of him.

"You are my mate, Va," Dom said, "and I will stay with you and protect you always."

Va said: "Yes, I will be your mate."

The sun broke through in the afternoon: the mists cleared and the lake drowsed under a hot blue sky. They swam in the cool waters and afterward lay together in the sun.

As the day ended, Va fed Bel and put him to rest

in his mossy bed. He looked up at her and she sang to him, one of the lullabies that her mother had sung to her. Dom came into the hut while she was singing and squatted beside her, listening. She smiled at Dom, and sang the song for him as well.

Dom and Va lived ever after in the hut beside the lake. Not always happily, not always peacefully: they had sorrows and they had disagreements. But always Dom remembered that Va was his mate and the mother of his children. And Va remembered all he had done for them and loved him, most of the time.

They had other children, girls as well as boys. They taught them the skills of planting and harvesting, of fishing and cattle herding. From Dom the boys learned to use clubs, to defend their home from attackers. From Va the children learned to love beauty and all beautiful things—to sing, and tell stories, and paint in bright colors.

Their children, or perhaps their children's children, learned to make boats so that they could fish in the lake more easily. As generations passed the village grew bigger. In time it became a town, in time a mighty city.

But this is the story of Dom and Va. In the dawn of human history, he was our father.

She was our mother.

In the Beginning
A Short Story Adaptation

MANY MANY YEARS AGO, TWO TRIBES LIVED in a very big country. One tribe lived in the north, and one tribe lived in the south. These tribes never met. The land between them was jungle and swamps. The men of the two tribes never went into the dark jungle, and they never went over the deep swamps.

The people of the south found fruit and nuts on the trees. They took seeds of grass and ground them. They ground them between two stones and made flour. They made bread from the flour. They took eggs from hens and milk from cows. They kept the hens and cows with them, so they got eggs and milk easily.

They kept some seeds and put them in the ground. Grass grew from the seeds. This grass had big seeds. They called it corn. They built huts near their corn fields and made a village. They planted trees near the huts, and they got fruit and nuts easily from them.

This was their home. At night they told stories and sang songs.

The people of the north did not have corn. They did not have bread or eggs or milk. They killed animals. They were good hunters.

They followed the deer and ran very fast. Some deer did not run very fast. The hunters killed those. Then they ate them.

These people did not have homes. They made nests, like birds, but the nests were not in the trees. They were on the ground, in the long grass. They slept in these nests at night. They did not tell stories. They did not sing songs.

The tribes lived like this for a very long time—for thousands of years. Day followed night. Summer followed winter. Year followed year. The people of the south and the people of the north learned new things.

The people in the south made tools from stones. They made knives and hammers out of stone. They made stone wheels, and they ground corn into flour with the wheels. They made pots. They baked the pots in fires, and then the pots were strong and held water. They made ovens and baked bread.

The people in the north did not have any tools. They killed the deer with their hands. They ate them and left the bones. One day a man looked at the leg bone of a deer. He hit things with it. He thought: "With this bone, my arm is strong." He went with the hunters, and he took the bone with him. He hit a deer on the head, and the deer fell. The hunters of the tribe took bones. They hit deer with them, and the deer fell. The hunters called them killing clubs.

The world changed. Summers grew cold, and winters grew very cold. There was ice on the rivers, and there were mountains of ice in the sea. Cold winds came from these ice mountains. Some animals died. Some moved to the south. They looked for warm weather and food.

The jungles died. The swamps changed. The people of the north followed the animals to the south. They took their killing clubs with them.

A boy called Dom lived in the northern tribe. He was tall and strong. He ran very fast in the hunt. He ran like the men. He had a long killing club. He rubbed it with sand. He rubbed it for a long time and made it white. It was bright in the sunlight. Dom used it in the hunt and killed a deer with it.

In the south the corn did not grow well. The people worked and worked, but they were cold. The cold winds cut them. They made clothes and put them on their bodies. They built huts with thick walls.

A girl called Va lived with the southern tribe. She was small and beautiful. She made pots and painted them. She made them well, and she painted bright pictures on them. She sang songs, and her voice was sweet.

The ice moved south, and the people of the north went in front of it. They went a very long way. They hunted animals. One day they found a large number of animals. These animals did not run like deer. The people of the north killed them easily. They made a feast.

Men attacked them at the feast. It was the men of the south. Why did they attack? Because the animals were their cows.

The men of the south attacked, but they did not have killing clubs. The men of the north drove them back. They ran back to their village. The northern men followed them.

There were thick bushes around the village. The southern men cut thorns and put them with the bushes. This made a wall of thorns around the village. There was a spring in the village. They got water from it. They kept food in the village too.

The northern men attacked the village. The thorns kept them back. Three or four men got through the wall, but the southern men killed them. The northern men went away.

They did not go far. They made a camp not far from the village. They had the killing clubs, and they were strong. They did not need a wall.

They attacked again, and the southern men drove them back. Day followed day. The northern men attacked the village again and again. But the wall of thorns was strong. Again and again the southern men drove back the attackers.

There was a forest near the village. It had big trees. It had a stream too. The stream fell from rocks into a pool. Trees leaned over the pool. Squirrels ran along the branches of the trees. Birds sat on the branches and sang.

Va loved the forest and the pool. She swam there on warm days. She sat on the rocks beside the pool, and she sang like the birds.

Va was in the village. She thought about the forest. She looked at the wall of thorns. In one place it was not very thick. She made a hole and crawled through it. She saw the camp of the northern people, and she did not go that way. She crawled through tall grass. She went slowly and quietly into the forest.

The stream ran over stones under the trees. Va walked beside the stream. There were bushes there with bright flowers. She took flowers and put them in her hair. The stream sang, and the birds sang in the branches. She was very happy.

She came to the place of rocks. The stream ran between the rocks and fell into the pool. The trees leaned over, but they did not hide the sky. The sky was blue and the sun shone. It shone on the pool and made the water bright.

Squirrels ran along the branches of the trees. They never hid from Va. One of them came down to the ground beside the pool. Va knew this squirrel. It came to her hand, and she gave some nuts to it. She was happy. She touched the squirrel gently and spoke gently to it.

Va stayed beside the pool a long time. The birds sang, and she sang too. She looked at her face in the water of the pool. The birds and the squirrels saw her, but people did not see her.

She left the pool and went through the forest. She crawled through the tall grass. She came to the wall of thorns and found the small hole. She crawled through it. She was back in her village.

Dom attacked the village with the men from the north. The thorns kept them out. They were very angry. They said: "We will get through the thorns. We will kill the people in the village."

Dom was angry and said this too. The northern men swung their clubs and danced a war dance. Dom danced with the men.

They attacked again, and the thorns kept them out again. They said: "We will wait. The people in the village will soon need food and water. They will come out, and we will kill them."

They killed the animals near the village. Soon there weren't any animals there. They hunted a long way from the village.

One day Dom fell on some stones in the hunt. He stood up, but he could not run. He could walk slowly, but he could not hunt with the men.

They left Dom with the young boys. He did not like that. He took his killing club and walked slowly through the tall grass. He did not go near the village. He saw the forest and went to it.

He found the stream and followed it. He walked in the stream. He saw the bushes with their bright flowers. He swung his club and hit the bushes. The flowers fell on the water. The stream carried them through the forest.

Dom was a good hunter. He moved very quietly, and he listened. He heard the song of the birds. He heard the squirrels on the branches. And he heard a new sound. It was a strange sound. He listened. It was a girl's voice. She sang a song. He did not know the song, but he liked the strange sound.

Dom walked very slowly. He was very quiet. He came to the place of rocks. He looked over the rocks and saw the pool. He saw Va, too. She sat by the pool and sang.

The flowers came down on the stream and fell into the pool. She leaned over and took them. She put the flowers in her hair. The flowers were very beautiful there. Va looked at her face and hair in the water. She was beautiful too.

Dom jumped down from the rocks. Va saw him. She said: "Who are you?"

Dom did not understand her words. He said: "Who are you?"

Va did not understand his words.

She saw the bone—the killing club. She knew then: he was one of the northern tribe.

Va was frightened. She stood up and ran through the forest.

Dom said: "Come back!"

She did not understand the words. She ran fast.

Dom could not run. He walked, and he hunted for her in the forest. He did not find her. He looked behind the trees and in the bushes. But he moved slowly, and he did not find her. In the end, he went back to his people.

Va was very frightened. She hid behind bushes. She heard Dom and saw him, but he did not see her. He went out of the forest. Then she went back to her village. She crawled through the tall grass. She crawled through the hole in the wall of thorns. The people did not see her.

The men of the village met around the fire. One man said:

"We have nearly eaten our food, and we cannot get food from our fields. Our enemies are there."

An old man said: "Our enemies cannot get through the wall of thorns. We have to wait a long time, so we have to use our food very slowly."

The first man said: "In the end we will not have any food. Then we will be hungry."

The old man said: "Our enemies will be hungry too. They have eaten our cows. They will be hungry, and they will go. We have to wait. They will go. Then we can go out of our village and get food."

Va was frightened. The boy in the forest was one of their enemies. She did not go to the forest again for a long time. She stayed in the village.

One day Dom went to the forest before daylight. He walked beside the stream and came to the pool. It was dark. The sun was not yet in the sky. One or two birds sang quietly.

Dom saw a big bush near the pool. He went behind the bush and lay on the ground there. In the hunt men waited for animals like that. They hid, and the animals came near them. Then they ran and killed them.

Dom waited for the girl. "Will she come?" he thought. He waited a long time. The sun came up. It shone far up in the sky. The birds sang. He saw squirrels on the branches of the trees. Dom lay quietly and did not move. He stayed behind the bush, and he waited.

Then the girl came. He saw her at the place of rocks. She jumped down. She looked around the place. She did not see Dom. He was behind the bush. She went to the pool. She sat beside the pool and looked into it.

Dom watched her. Then he stood up very quietly.

He walked very quietly to the girl. He was behind her—very near her, but she could not see him.

Va looked into the water. She saw her face. Then she saw a second face. It was Dom's. She was very frightened.

She jumped up and ran through the forest. She ran very fast, but Dom was a hunter. Very soon he caught her. He held her in his arms. She fought, but he held her.

Dom said: "I have caught you, but do not be frightened. I will not hurt you."

She did not understand his words, but his voice was not angry. He said again: "I will not hurt you."

Then she did not fight, and Dom did not hold her.

The next day, Dom went to the forest again. He went to the place of rocks and the pool. He saw Va beside the pool. He called to her: "I am here. Dom." She was not frightened. She smiled at him. He went to her and sat beside her.

In the evening, Va went back to the village. She crawled through the hole under the wall. A man saw her. He took her to the old men of the tribe.

He said: "She went out of the village. She made

a hole under the wall. There was not a hole before that. Our enemies can come through the hole."

The old men were angry. They said to Va's father: "Watch her. Keep her in the hut."

Va's father took her to the hut and told her mother. Her mother was very angry. She said: "You have to stay in the hut, Va. You will work there, and I will watch you. You will not go out of the village again."

Va was sad. The next day, she was very sad—very, very sad. Dom was in the forest, but she could not go there. She stayed in the hut, and her mother watched her.

Night came. Va went out of the hut very quietly. She went to the wall. The hole was not there now. There were just thorns. The thorns hurt her. She could not get out. She went back to the hut and cried.

Dom went to the forest. He called Va, but he did not get an answer. He walked beside the stream to the place of rocks. She was not there. Dom sat on the rocks and waited. Va did not come.

He walked through the forest. He called Va's name. He listened—the birds answered, but Va's voice did not. He took flowers from the bushes. He dropped the flowers in the stream. The stream took them.

Dom came out of the forest. He saw the village with its wall of thorns. Va was in the village, but she was a long way from him.

He went back through the forest. The birds sang. The squirrels ran along the branches. The red and yellow flowers were on the bushes. But the forest was not the same. Va was not there.

The next day Dom went to the forest again. He did not find Va. He looked for her and called her. Then he went back slowly to his people.

There was a meeting of the men. Dom sat down and listened. One man said: "We cannot get into the village. The wall of thorns is very strong."

A second man said: "There are not any animals here now. We hunt a long way from here, and we do not find deer easily. It is not good here. We have to leave this place."

The chief hunter said: "Should we leave this place? What do you say?"

Some men said, "Leave!" But some men said, "Attack the village again!"

Dom sat with the men. He heard their words but he did not speak. He was young, and young men did not speak.

A man said: "The village is at the bottom of a hill. There are big stones on the hill. A big stone killed my brother. It rolled down a hill and killed him. We can roll a stone down this hill. It will go through the wall of thorns, and then we can go into the village easily."

The chief hunter said: "Can we move the stones? The ground holds them."

A man said: "The ground in front of a stone holds it. We can dig the ground away from there. Then we can move the stone."

The chief hunter asked: "Should we do this?"

The men said: "Yes!"

They found a very big stone on the hill. They dug the ground away from the front with their fingers. The work was hard.

Dom worked with the men. He looked at the forest.

He thought: "Is Va in the forest now?"

A man said: "Work, boy!" Dom worked.

They worked and worked. They pushed the stone, but the stone did not move. They were very tired. They were hungry too. They needed food.

At night some men said: "This is not good. We have to leave this place. We need food. We have to hunt."

The chief hunter said: "We have to work again. We will move the stone in the morning."

In the morning they went back to the hill. They worked again. They dug the ground away with their fingers. The stone moved. It was a very big stone. The men stood behind it. They pushed, and the stone moved again. It rolled down the hill.

It did not roll far. It stopped, and they pushed again. The stone stopped again and again. The men were very tired.

The chief hunter said, "Push!"

Some men were angry and said: "We are tired and hungry. We have to leave this place. We need food. We have to hunt."

But the chief hunter was strong. He said again: "Push!"

They pushed, and the stone moved.

This time it did not stop. It rolled down the hill.

It went fast. The men ran after it. They gave the hunters' cry.

The stone rolled very fast. It rolled into the wall of thorns. It went through the wall and rolled into the village. The northern men ran behind it. There was a hole in the wall now. They went through the hole. They were in the village.

The southern men came out of their huts. They fought the northern men.

It was a hard fight. The southern men fought for their homes. They fought well. But they did not have killing clubs. The northern men had killing clubs. With their clubs they were strong.

Dom fought with the northern men. A southern man bit his arm with his teeth. Dom hit the southern man with his club. The man fell down. A second man ran at Dom. Dom hit him too.

There were fires near the huts. They had pots on them. A southern man jumped at Dom, and Dom rolled into one of the fires. The fire hurt his leg. Hot water from a pot fell on his chest.

Dom cried out. He was very angry. He got up and hit the man with his club. The man fell and did not get up.

The end of the fight came soon. The northern men killed the southern men. They gave the hunters' cry and danced the war dance. Dom danced with them.

The women and children of the southern tribe were frightened. They hid in the huts. The northern men pulled them out of the huts. The women and children cried.

The northern men said: "Food! We want food!" The women did not understand the words. The northern men put their hands to their mouths. The women knew the meaning of that. They brought food to the northern men.

Va was very frightened. Her father was dead. Her two brothers were dead. The northern men were angry. She brought bread. They did not know bread, and they ate it with angry noises.

She saw Dom. There was blood on his hands. His killing club was in his hands, and there was blood on the killing club too.

She thought: "He killed my father and my brothers."

Dom saw her and spoke. He spoke gently, but she did not smile. She turned away. She hated Dom.

Dom said: "You are not hurt, Va. I am happy."

She did not look at him. He said: "I will look after you."

She did not understand. She said: "You killed my father and my brothers. I hate you."

He did not understand her words but he knew her meaning.

The northern men made a feast. They said: "We are strong in war! We killed our enemies. Now we will take their cows and their homes. We will take their women too. They will be our wives."

Dom said to Va: "You will be my wife. I will look after you."

She did not understand the words. She did not look at him.

A big hunter came. He said to Dom: "You cannot have a wife. You are just a boy. This girl will be my wife."

Dom said: "She is my girl."

The man laughed at him. Dom fought the man. But the man was very big and strong. He hit Dom with his club, and Dom fell down.

The hunter pushed Va into a hut. He said: "This is my hut. You will be my wife." Va knew the meaning. She was very sad. She cried in the hut.

The northern men ate and ate. Then they slept. Dom did not eat. He did not sleep. He was sad and angry.

He looked for Va. He found her in the hut. She was sad and angry too. He spoke, but she turned away.

He spoke very gently. He said: "Come with me." He pulled her arm, and he looked out of the hut.

Va knew the meaning. "I hate him," she thought. "He killed my father and my brothers. But the big man is a very hard man. I will go with Dom. Then I will run away."

In the morning they were very hungry. Va found a tree with fruit. She and Dom took the fruit from the branches and ate it. Then they walked again.

They walked and walked. Va found fruit and nuts for them. One day they were on a hill. Dom saw deer at the bottom of the hill. He went down the hill quietly. The deer saw him, and they were frightened. They ran away. Dom ran too.

The deer and Dom went very far. Va could not see them. She thought: "Now I can run away. Dom will not find me. Dom killed my father and my brothers with his club."

But she did not run away. She thought: "Where will I go? I do not have a home now. I do not have any people."

Dom killed a young deer with his club. He carried it back to Va.

He said: "Here is some meat. We will eat it."

Va found sticks. Dom said: "What are you doing?"

She said: "I am going to make a fire." Dom did not understand the words. He watched her.

Va made a fire with sticks. She put the meat on the fire and cooked it. Dom said: "I like the smell."

Va gave some meat to him. He said: "It is very good. Eat, Va."

Va knew the meaning. She was hungry. She ate the meat with him.

Day followed day. Still they went on. Sometimes Va found nuts or fruit for food. Sometimes Dom killed animals. Often they were hungry.

Dom talked to Va. She knew some of the words. She did not speak often to Dom. She was still angry with him.

Va hated the killing club. She looked for fruit and nuts. But often she could not find them. Then she ate Dom's meat.

Sometimes they saw people a long way from them. Dom and Va did not go to them. They were just Dom and Va. They did not have a tribe.

One day Va looked for fruit in a forest. She found bushes with flowers. There was a stream. Dom was not there. She sat beside the stream and sang.

Dom heard her voice. He went through the forest and found her. He said: "Your song is beautiful."

The song stopped. Dom said: "Sing for me, Va." She did not sing. Dom said: "You are beautiful too."

Dom took flowers from a bush. He gave them to Va. He said: "Put them in your hair, Va."

She dropped the flowers on the ground.

Dom was angry. He hit her face with his hand. Va looked at him. Then she turned away.

Dom said: "I am sorry, Va." Va understood the words. She did not answer.

Dom was not happy now. He said: "We have to go away from here." Va did not speak. Dom went away. Va followed him.

One day Dom was ill. He shivered. His body was heavy. He could not run. Then he could not walk. Dom lay down. He was very ill. First he was very hot; then he was very cold and he shivered. He said: "I am dying."

Va went away. Dom could not get up. He thought: "She will leave me now."

Va looked for herbs. She found them and brought them back. Dom was asleep. She made a fire with sticks.

Dom woke up. He said: "You are still here, Va. Now I am happy."

Va gave the herbs to him. Dom asked: "What should I do?" She said: "Eat them." Dom ate the herbs. The fire was bright, but Dom was still cold. He shivered. Va held him in her arms. He said: "That is good, Va." She did not answer.

Soon Dom was well. He said: "You looked after me, and now I am well, Va." She did not answer. He said: "We can go on now."

They came to a lake. The water was quiet. It was very beautiful.

Va looked at the place beside the lake. She thought: "We can build a hut here. We can plant corn. We can make a home."

But she did not speak. Dom said: "There aren't any deer in this place. We have to go on."

They went on and left the lake behind them.

They came to high land. There were trees and bushes.

Dom killed a deer. Va made a fire and cooked the meat. They ate. Then Dom went away. He needed a drink. There was a stream not very far from them. Dom went to the stream and drank.

Va stayed near the fire. She heard a sound and looked up. She saw a big animal. It lay on the branch of a tree. It was yellow and black. Its eyes were bright and green. Its teeth were bright too. It was a leopard.

Va was very frightened. The leopard moved and showed its teeth. She cried out.

Dom heard her cry. He ran back from the stream. He saw the leopard. He was frightened too, but he did not run away. He stood in front of Va.

The leopard jumped out of the tree. It jumped on Dom, and he fell under it. Its claws tore Dom's arm. He pulled away from the leopard. His arm hurt, and there was blood on it. He took up his killing club.

The leopard jumped at him again. Dom swung his club. The club hit the leopard's head. The leopard's claws tore Dom's side, but the leopard was hurt. It made an angry sound, but it went away.

Blood came out of Dom's arm and side. Va found herbs. She held them on his arm and side. She held them there for a long time. In the end, the blood stopped.

Dom said: "Thank you, Va. With your help I am well now."

Va thought: "You saved me from the leopard, Dom." But she did not speak the words. She thought: "You saved me from the leopard, but you killed my father and my brothers. I hate you."

One day Va spoke to Dom. She said: "I am going to stay here."

She spoke with his words. Dom said: "No. We will go on. I can't find deer here easily."

Va said: "I am going to stay, Dom."

Dom said: "I will go on, and you will come with me."

Va looked at him. "I will not come."

Dom said: "Why? Why won't you come?"

Va said: "I am heavy."

Dom said: "I was heavy, and you gave herbs to me. I will find herbs for you."

Va said: "No. I do not need herbs. I am not ill. I am going to have a baby."

Dom was very happy. He said: "I will have a son!"

Va said: "He will be my son."

Dom said: "What do you want, Va? Just tell me, and you can have it. You are my wife."

Va said: "I want a home for my son. There were huts in my village. I want a hut."

Dom said: "I can't make a hut."

Va said: "I will show you."

She showed him, and Dom made the hut. He put long sticks in the ground. He put branches on top of the sticks and at the sides. Then he put big leaves and grass over the branches.

It was a good hut. Va stayed there. Dom went away and found food. He brought food to Va. There was a stream near the hut. She got water from the stream.

One day Dom came back with food. He heard a strange sound. It was a cry. He went into the hut. It was not Va's cry. In her arms there was a baby.

Dom took the baby. He said: "This is my son." He was very happy.

The baby cried. Va said: "Give him back to me." Dom gave the baby back to Va.

It was summer. The baby grew big and strong. Dom found food for them. Sometimes he went far away.

Va took water from the stream. Dom was away. She made a fire. It was a big fire, and very hot. Va found clay. She made a pot and baked it in the fire. Then she carried water in the pot.

Va found grass near the hut. It was like corn. She took seeds from the grass. She ground the seeds on a stone. She made flour and baked bread.

Dom came back with meat and fruit. Va gave some bread to him. Dom said: "It is good. There are good things here. There is bread. There is the hut. There is my son. And there is you, Va."

Va did not speak. Dom said: "Sing for me, Va." But Va did not sing.

Dom went away again. He hunted far away. Va

was happy with her baby. She had bread and water. There was some fruit near the hut. She found fish in the stream. She took some fish and cooked them in the fire and ate them.

Va loved her baby. She called him Kin. She thought: "Maybe Dom won't come back. Then there will be just Kin and me." She was very happy.

But Dom came back. He took the baby in his arms. He was happy too. He said: "You are my son." And he laughed.

Va did not laugh. She thought: "Dom killed my father and my brothers." She took the baby from Dom. She thought: "This is *my* son."

Fall came, and the leaves were brown. They fell from the branches. The days grew short.

Dom said: "The deer are going far away. We have to follow them." Va said: "You can follow them. Kin is very small. He and I will stay here."

Dom said: "Then I will not go away. I will hunt the deer, but I will bring the meat back to you."

It was cold again. Va made a fire in the hut. She put the skins of animals on Kin. There weren't any grass seeds now, but she found roots in the ground and cooked them.

Dom brought back meat. They ate some meat, and they made some dried meat over the fire. Dom said: "There are not any deer near here now. I have to go away and hunt. I will be away a long time, but I will bring food back to you."

Day followed day, and Dom did not come back. Va thought: "Maybe now he won't come back." There was some dried meat in the hut. There were fish in the stream, and there were roots in the ground. She had a hut and a fire and her baby. She was very happy.

One day Va went out. She looked for roots in the ground.

She heard a sound and looked up. She saw two men. They were big and strong. Their faces were hard. They had killing clubs.

Va thought: "They will hurt my baby."

She ran away. She did not run to the hut; she ran away from it. The men followed her. They ran very fast. Soon one of them caught her. He took her hair and pulled her to the ground.

The men made angry sounds at Va. She did not understand them, but their voices were hard. She was very frightened. She thought: "Maybe they will kill me. Maybe they will take me with them. Then my baby will die." She fought.

The man tore her hair and hit her with his club. She thought: "Dom is far away." But she called his name. The man hit her again. She called out in a strong voice: "Dom! Help me!"

Dom went a long way from the hut and hunted. In the end he found a deer and killed it with his club. He put the deer on his back and carried it.

He saw the two men. He thought: "They will take the deer from me." So he hid in some bushes and watched them. The men did not see him. They went on. He put the deer on his back again.

Dom saw smoke in the sky. It was the smoke from Va's fire. He was happy. He thought: "Soon I will be home."

Then he thought: "Those men will see the smoke too. They will find the fire. They will find Va and the baby. They will hurt them."

He was tired but he ran.

He heard Va's cry—"Dom! Help me!"—and he dropped the deer and ran fast.

He saw the two men and Va. The men saw him too. They turned and swung their killing clubs.

Dom was not frightened; he was very angry. He ran to them. He swung his club.

Dom moved very quickly. He hit one man on the head. The man fell down. The second man hit Dom. They fought.

The second man was very strong. He hit Dom's club with his club. Dom's club fell from his hand. The man swung his club at Dom. Dom put up his arm. The club hit Dom's arm and he fell down.

The man stood over Dom. Va was behind him. She jumped at the man. He fell beside Dom. Dom got up quickly. He took his club again and hit the man.

That man died. The first man got up and ran away.

Dom did not follow him. He said to Va: "Are you well, Va?"

Va said: "Yes Dom." She said: "You saved me." She spoke the words this time. She said: "You saved me and our son."

They went back to the hut. Kin was asleep. Dom took him in his arms. He said: "He is well."

Va said to Dom: "You are strong and good, Dom. You saved us. I will be your wife."

That night they sat in the hut. The fire was warm. Va cooked meat in the pot. They sat close together and ate the meat.

Va sang, and Dom listened. She sang to Kin. She sang to Dom too. She did not think: "Dom killed my father." She thought: "He is strong and good." She smiled at Dom. She was very happy.

It was cold in winter. But they had a fire in the hut. They had skins from animals. Dom brought back food.

Spring came. Then summer. Year followed year. People came to that place. They were good people. They built huts near Dom's hut. In the end there was a village there.

These people grew corn and made bread. They had tools. The men were hunters. The women looked after them and the children. The women told stories and sang songs. The new tribe grew.

Kin grew tall like Dom but his face was like Va's face.

Dom said: "He will be a very good hunter. I will show him. He will have my club. He will become the leader of our tribe."

Va did not answer. She made pots. Kin watched her. He asked: "Can I do that?" Va showed him. She sang songs and Kin listened. He sang those songs too.

Dom said to Va: "Our son is beautiful—like you."

Va said: "He is good and strong—like you."

They loved their son. They were very happy.

Their names were Dom and Va. Dom of the north and Va of the south. And through them the two tribes became one tribe many, many years ago.

Read on for a peek at another adventure
from John Christopher!

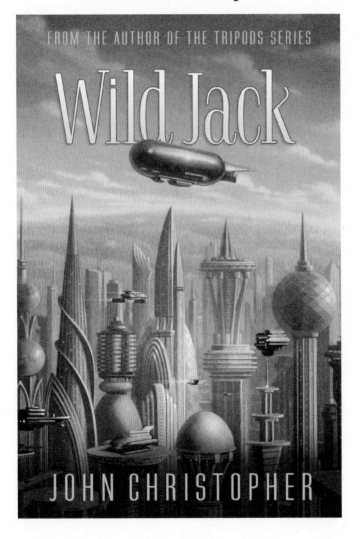

I WOKE UP TO THE SOUND OF HUMMING, LIKE that of an enormous bee whose wings you might think filled the sky. I did not need to look at my watch to know it was eight o'clock. Today was Wednesday, and that was the Rome airship coming in to land.

Yawning, I stretched but did not get up right away. The windows facing my bed took up the full length of the wall, and I could lie and look out over the parks and buildings of London. In the foreground was the garden of our house, extending for more than a hundred yards in patterns of lawn and shrubbery, flower beds, and cunningly designed streams and pools. The gardeners were already at work.

Beyond, divided from the garden by a high fence covered with climbing roses, lay St. James's Park, at this time quiet and empty. In the distance I could just see a corner of the Palace, which was the seat of government for the city. My father was a member of the council, which met there, though at the moment he and my mother were away, on holiday in the Mediterranean.

In the opposite direction stood the huge funnel shape of the airport. The humming grew louder as the airship descended toward it, then cut off as it sank beneath the containing walls. I should not have heard it at all, of course, if my windows had not been opened—my room was sound-proofed and air-conditioned—but I rather liked the noise. I also liked waking to the smell of growing things, new-mown grass and flowers. The air-conditioner had a scent console incorporated in it which could have provided much the same effect, but I never thought it got things quite right.

The day was fine. Sunlight lit the scene outside

and slanted through my windows, sharpening the blues and reds of the Persian carpet beside my bed. That was enough in itself to justify feeling cheerful, but I was aware of a sense of anticipation as well. I remembered: Miranda.

She was a cousin of mine, or, to be accurate, her father and mine were cousins. The Sherrins lived in Southampton, seventy miles from London. They had lived in London some years earlier, and Mr. Sherrin and my father had been political rivals. I knew nothing about the causes of their disagreement, but it had been serious. There had apparently been a lot of argument and debate, with people taking sides. In the end it had come to an issue in the council, where my father had won. To clinch matters, Mr. Sherrin's opponents had voted him into exile.

My father had not wanted that and in the years since then had worked to have the order of banishment revoked. He had succeeded a few months earlier. The Sherrins had not yet decided whether or not to return permanently to London, but my parents had suggested that they make use of our house while they themselves were away on holiday. So they had come up from Southampton and brought Miranda with them.

She was a few months younger than I, and I remembered her as a thin plain girl with not a great deal to say for herself. I discovered she had changed a lot. She still did not talk much, though what she did say was in a cool low voice that made you want to listen. In other respects she was very different. Her hair was longer, silky, and more golden than I remembered, and her face was fuller, but with attractive hollows under high cheekbones. There was her smile, too, which was harder to describe: slow and strange. It was rare, but worth waiting for.

I decided to get up and pressed the button by my bed which would flash a call signal in the servants' quarters. It was very quiet now that the airship had landed, with only the small distant sounds of the gardeners. I wondered how many people had come from Rome: not many, probably. People did not travel much between the cities. Why should they, since one place was so much like another? There was no reason to leave one's home city except to go on holiday, and no one was likely to want to go on holiday to another city.

The bell on my door pinged softly and I called, "Come in." My manservant, Bobby, crossed the room to my bed.

"Good morning, young sir. I trust you slept well. What would you like for breakfast today?"

He listened and nodded as I gave my orders, then went to run my bath and put out my clothes to wear, asking me which shirt I preferred. Before leaving to fetch my breakfast, he said, "Is there anything else, young sir?"

I shook my head. "No, boy!"

Bobby had been my manservant since I came out of the nursery. He was more than three times my age.

White clouds drifted in from the west but the morning stayed bright, and after breakfast I took Miranda down to the river. Our boathouse on the Thames was close to the Houses of Parliament, which had once been the center of government but was now a museum. It was not much visited: I saw servant-attendants there, but no one else.

We met Gary at the boathouse. He and I were in the same class at school and slept in the same dormitory. We were friends after a fashion, though we did seem to spend a lot of time fighting. Usually I won. We were about the same height, but he was thinner than I was and less strong.

"You're late," he said.

That was true; Miranda had taken a long time getting ready. I paid no attention to him and led the way into the boathouse.

There were four boats in the slips. One was the family cabin cruiser, another was my father's speedboat, and a third belonged to my mother. The fourth was mine, a present for my last birthday. According to the regulations, I was not old enough to take a powerboat out on the river, but my father had managed to fix things for me.

It was an eight-foot dinghy, bright red, with a small but quite powerful motor. The boathouse servant made it ready, unplugging the powerline through which the batteries had been charged and connecting the batteries to the engine. He saluted me and handed over.

She was called "Sea Witch." I was not entirely satisfied with the name and thought occasionally of changing it. In the last day or two it had crossed my mind that "Miranda" might be a good name for a boat.

I eased her from the slip into the channel and so out of the boathouse into the river. With Miranda and Gary standing on either side of me, I opened up the throttle and took her down river. There were quite a lot of small craft about. Over the high-pitched hum of the engine I asked Miranda about Southampton: did people there do much boating?

She shook her head, the wind tumbling her yellow hair. "Not as much as here. Of course, there's much less river within the wall. The Outlands are nearer to us than they are to you."

"The Outlands" was the name for everything outside the boundaries of the cities and the holiday islands. There were roads running through them linking the civilized places, and the ground was kept clear for fifty yards or so on either side of the roads. Beyond that, nature ran riot, chiefly in forest.

Savages lived in the Outlands. They occasionally tried to attack cars on the roads, but usually without success since the cars traveled too fast to be damaged by a stone or two thrown by a few barbarians. If they attempted to mass in large numbers or put up barriers or obstacles, electronic monitors gave a warning to the nearest control unit. It was easy enough then to send an airship to deal with them.

But here we were in the heart of London, one of the biggest cities in the world, and the Outlands seemed very remote. On either bank of the Thames we saw buildings spaced among patches of green. I recalled a picture I had seen of Old London, with the houses packed close together, row on row of them, close-crammed and full of people—millions of people swarming like ants. Today we numbered ourselves in a few thousand. I tried to think about a million people—a thousand times a thousand—but it was beyond imagining.

In the distance, across open ground, I could see our house and even make out the small turret room which was my father's study. To the right was the airport funnel, with an airship at this moment rising out of it. That one was starting on the long route to Delhi. I knew the times of all the scheduled flights.

The energy tower stood farther to the right still, a slender shaft rising high into the sky. It was clad in anodized aluminum which reflected the sun so that it gleamed like a tower of gold—which in a way it was, because the energy tower generated and dispensed the power which kept the city alive. Everything depended on it: this small boat as much as the automat factories. The power line in the boat house ran back to the energy tower.

Airships had their own nuclear motors, but everything else came from the towers. The cars which traveled between the cities were powered by fuel cells which had to be charged at regular intervals. Each city had its own energy tower, but the London tower was the biggest in England.

I drove the boat between two pillars, the remains of an old bridge, and we came out into the wider stretch of the London docks. They had no use any longer; air freighters carried what trade there was in and out of the city.

It must have been a strange place in the old days, with the great ships rising high above the water, the air loud with the cries of stevedores, the clank of steel, the hoarse shrieks of steam whistles. We traveled now through silence and emptiness. I saw a solitary speedboat in the distance, that was all. Not many people came to this section of the river, disliking it for the bare wideness of its waters.

Gary held the same view and said so. This was boring. Why didn't we go to the pleasure gardens on the south bank? There would be something to do there.

I asked Miranda: "What do you think? Would you rather go to the pleasure gardens?"

She shook her head slightly. "I like it here."

I took the boat under high walls of gray stone, hiding the sun. We came to a flight of worn steps, and I tied up to a rusting metal ring. I helped Miranda out, and Gary and I followed her up the steps to the top. We came into sunshine again and sprawled on the warm stone, Gary and I carelessly and Miranda neatly. She was wearing lime-green trousers with a primrose-yellow blouse, and she hugged her knees with clasped hands.

I said: "I came here once on my own and stayed till after dark. It was a bit weird: the gray of the sky and the river getting darker all the time and no sound apart from the lap of waves and a seagull. I could almost imagine I saw a ghost liner coming in from the estuary."

"Some imagination." Gary laughed. "What a nut!"

Miranda said quietly, "I can understand that. It's a strange atmosphere, even in daylight." She smiled. "I don't think I would have had the nerve to stay here alone after dark."

"Two nut cases," Gary said. But he sounded more resentful than contemptuous.

Mr. Sherrin appeared in the sitting room while I was waiting for Miranda that evening, and I put down the magazine I had been glancing through. He said, "That's all right, Clive. Don't let me interrupt you."

I shook my head. "I wasn't reading. Just passing the time."

The magazine was called *Twent-Cent* and carried stories and picture strips about the past, before the Breakdown. They were mostly lurid accounts of violence and crime, and at one time I had been keen on them. But one felt differently as one grew older; they were really meant for a younger age group than mine. I was a little ashamed of being found looking at the magazine at all.

Mr. Sherrin smiled. "Waiting for Miranda? You'll need plenty to occupy your time if you're going to make a habit of that."

He was tall and gray-haired, with a face that, except for being thinner, resembled my father's: both had bushy eyebrows and rather long noses. But there was also a difference in expression, which I suppose you might sum up by saying that my father was a laughing man, Mr. Sherrin a smiling one. His smile was quiet and humorous, seeming to indicate someone who took a cool look at people and situations and the world in general. It was a bit like Miranda's, when I came to think of it.

My father's laughter, on the other hand, appeared to stem from a greater energy and boisterousness. Quietness was characteristic of Mr. Sherrin, but my father was most himself in doing something or saying something—the latter generally loudly and to an accompaniment of expansive gestures. I had occasionally found this trying. It was not that I was ashamed of my father—I was very proud of him—but there had been moments when I wished he could go about things a little less noisily.

I made some fumbling reply to the remark about Miranda, and Mr. Sherrin said, "Where are you off to this evening, anyway? The theater?"

I shook my head. "Only a party."

"Anyone I know?" He smiled again. "I'm a bit out of touch with London society, of course."

The drily humorous comment was, I thought, typical of him.

I said, "Brian Grantham. His parents are away as well—in the Hebrides, I think."

"Michael Grantham would be his father?" I nodded. "Yes, I remember him."

He was silent after that. I wondered if Brian's father had also been mixed up in the events leading up to the banishment—and one of those, perhaps, who had wanted the ban continued. But it wasn't something I could ask questions about.

Miranda appeared at last and we could go. Mr. Sherrin put music on as we left—Mozart or something similar. In my father's case it would have been Tchaikovsky or more likely Gilbert & Sullivan. He had an infuriating habit of whistling Sullivan tunes off-key.

We took a taxi—open, because it was a clear warm evening—to the Granthams' house, which was also on the north bank but farther west—not far from the wall, in fact. Brian, who had asked us, was at the same school as Gary and I, but a couple of years older. He had never invited either of us before, and I was fairly sure I knew why he had done so this time. The reason sat beside me, looking beautiful in a crimson dress.

A dozen or more were there already, boys and girls of Brian's age. There was the usual food and drink, dancing, and chatter. We were outside in the garden, and as the evening darkened, colored lamps lit up in the branches of trees all round. Occasionally there was also the light of a passing boat on the river. Music came from a number of speakers, and in quiet passages one could hear the splash of water.

We were drinking a light sparkling wine, and supplies ran out. A servant who looked about seventy came shuffling out with more. Someone called, "Get a move on, boy! We don't want to have to wait all night."

"Beg pardon, young sir."

He attempted to open a bottle with uncertain fingers, but the one who had spoken, Martin, said, "Leave it, boy, and totter away. I'll see to it."

The servant retreated, with another mumbled apology, and Martin started opening the bottle.

When the servant was out of earshot, Brian said, "Was that necessary?"

His voice was low but angry. Martin looked at him.

"What?"

"Talking that way to him. It's not his fault if he's old."

Martin laughed. "Perhaps not. Your parents' fault having him around, maybe. What's wrong with the rest home?"

The rest home was for old and sick servants, a kind of hospital. Food and shelter were provided, but not much in the way of extra comforts. There were usually plenty of vacancies; the servants who went there tended not to live very long.

"If you don't know," Brian said, "I don't suppose I could tell you." I was surprised how angry he was. "Anyway, he's our servant and I'll tell him what to do. And I don't like hearing him called 'boy.'"

Martin stared at him. "What's got into you? They're always called 'boy.'"

"Then it's about time they weren't. They're human beings, like us."

"Like us? Sure. Maybe we should fetch and carry

for them, turn about. And have one or two of them on the council."

There was some laughter.

Brian said, "It might not be a bad idea, at that. What right do we have to make them serve us?"

The laughter stopped; I imagine the others were as shocked as I was. The division between masters and servants was something we had taken for granted all our lives—something you did not even need to think about. Nor want to. A remark like that gave one an uncomfortable, crawly feeling. Brian had probably drunk too much wine, but that didn't justify it. Martin merely turned away, and no one else said anything. We all wanted to drop the subject, but Brian insisted on going on.

"Have you ever thought about how they came to be servants in the first place?"

Martin turned back and looked at him in exasperation. He said dismissively, "What needs thinking about? Because they're descendants of savages, that's why. They wanted to come into the cities to get away from the Outlands, and our ancestors let them. In the Outlands they would be just about scraping a miserable living if they weren't killed by wild beasts first. With us they have food and clothing and shelter. They made the bargain."

"Their great-grandfathers made the bargain," Brian said. "Does that bind them?"

The question was too absurd to need an answer.

Brian went on, "And what about the time before that—before there were savages at all?"

"They've always been savages."

"No, they haven't. Only since the Breakdown."

Martin shrugged. Before the Breakdown were the Dark Ages—millennia of squalid barbarism, followed by the two centuries of the technological explosion which were as bad if not worse. We all knew that. For two hundred years mankind, suddenly given machines and power, had squandered the resources of energy, burning up coal and oil recklessly, with no thought for the future. Then the oil supplies had failed and the coal seams had become too thin for economic working. As a result the complex structure of the early twenty-first century had fallen apart in wars and rebellions and men fighting for crusts of bread among rusting machines.

People had died in the millions and tens of millions. Only a handful—our ancestors—had had the courage and determination and intelligence to start building again in the midst of chaos. The organizers had been those scientists with an understanding of the techniques of nuclear energy. They knew that although it had been inadequate in keeping the whole world with its billions of inhabitants running, it could be used to power individual strongholds. So, one by one, the cities rose again, though far fewer and smaller, each centered about its energy tower. Beyond their walls stretched the Outlands, abandoned to the murderous whims of nature.

Brian seemed blind and deaf to the effect he was having. He said, "The reason the people of the Outlands became savages was because they were kept out of the cities. If they could have come in, they would have, and lived civilized lives. Those who tried were driven away, slaughtered."

"But if they had been let in," a girl said, "things would have been impossible. Everything was balanced on a knife edge. Any increase in numbers would have meant civilization breaking down again and us all becoming savages. Is that what you think should have happened?"

"There was a case for exclusion *then*," Brian said. "I'm not disputing that. But what about later? What about now? We have more food, more energy, more everything than we need. The cities could support ten times as many people as they do."

"So we could live in mobs again, like in the twentieth century?" That was another boy, Roland. "Let's bring the savages in and live alongside them in tenement buildings—is that what you want?"

"No, of course I don't." Brian suddenly seemed to realize the absurdity into which his argument had led him, and looked uncertain. "Anyway, I was talking about servants, really. They've lived in the cities for generations. We call them servants, but if we were honest we would call them slaves. They're born in slavery, live in slavery, die in slavery. In ancient Rome slaves had a slim chance of getting their freedom. Our servants have no hope at all."

There was a general murmur of disgust. The reference to ancient Rome had something to do with it. No one was interested in the Dark Ages, either early or late. And it wasn't true about slavery. Servants were paid money for their work—not a lot, it was true, but too much, many said, for the amount they did. "Slave" was an unpleasant expression which had no place in the civilized world of the twenty-third century.

Martin said, "You're just talking rubbish, Brian. The servants don't mind being servants, any more than the savages mind being savages. They're used to it—contented, in fact."

Brian asked, "How do you know?"

Roland said, "*I* know something. I know I've had enough of this talk. I mind that. Let's have some more music."

"You won't think," Brian said. "None of you will. That's the trouble—you won't let yourselves think."

"I'll tell you what I think," Martin said. "I think you should shut up, Brian, or else do the thing properly and go out and join Wild Jack."

That raised a laugh. We could all remember being told stories about Wild Jack by our nurses when we were little: Wild Jack, the bogeyman who would creep up from the Outlands, steal over the wall by night, and take back naughty children to his lair among the savages. Martin's remark reduced the subject to the level of the ridiculous, which was its proper place. Brian made a feeble attempt to continue with his protests, but no one was listening any longer.

After all, what point was there in talking about the Dark Ages or the savages, far away either in time or space? Servants brought out more food and drink. The sky was black above, but the lamps shone gaily in the trees. It was still warm, but if the evening were to turn cold, thermostats would switch on the heaters. A long boat, lit up from stem to stern, drifted past on the river, and farther off I heard the high whine of a speedboat.

The Outlands, we knew, were wild and trackless, inhabited by hungry, murdering savages, but all that was on the far side of the wall. We were snug in the city. I saw a high light in the distance, marking the summit of the energy tower.

Someone had turned up the music, and couples joined together to dance. Brian had seemingly accepted defeat and now had other things in mind. He came over and asked Miranda for a dance.

She gave him a small, cool smile. "I'm sorry. Clive's already asked me."

I hadn't, in fact, but I didn't argue about that. I

took her out onto the circle of polished wood, laid down by the servants between the trees. For the first time I felt there had been some point in the grinding tedium of dancing lessons. She danced lightly, humming in tune to the music. It was good to hold her and see her face close to mine in the lamplight.